THE MAN WHO CAME UPTOWN

GEORGE PELECANOS

ORION

An Orion paperback

First published in Great Britain in 2018
by Orion Fiction
This paperback edition published in 2019
by Orion Fiction,
an imprint of The Orion Publishing Group Ltd,
Carmelite House, 50 Victoria Embankment
London EC4Y 0DZ

An Hachette UK Company

1 3 5 7 9 10 8 6 4 2

A CIP catalogue record for this book is
available from the British Library.

ISBN (Mass Market Paperback) 978 1 4091 7974 0

Printed in Great Britain by Clays Ltd, Elcograf S.p.A

www.orionbooks.co.uk

'Perhaps the greatest living American crime writer'
Stephen King

'Triple-distilled excellence. Pelecanos is the undisputed
laureate of America's most secret city. Not just recom-
ded: this is essential reading' Lee Child

erful' Michael Connelly

ve the way he writes: economical, rhythmic, elliptical
angrily political' Val McDermid

Every time I read one of George Pelecanos's novels I'm
little awed and a little envious. The guy's a national
ire' Dennis Lehane

ican crime writing at its finest' *Independent on Sunday*

anos is a powerful writer - he deserves to be listed
g the best' *Observer*

-standard character-driven crime writing that few will
atch' *Financial Times*

orge Pelecanos writes hard-boiled fiction with heart'
Sunday Telegraph

GEORGE PELECANOS is a bestselling and award-winning author, independent-film producer and essayist. He was a producer and Emmy-nominated writer on HBO series *The Wire*, *Treme* and, most recently, *The Deuce*. He lives in Maryland with his wife and three children.

Find out more by visiting his website:
www.george-pelecanos.com

*To Charles Willeford and
Elmore Leonard*

PART I

ONE

WHEN ANTONIUS thought of all the things they'd done wrong the day of the robbery, wearing hoodies might have been at the top of the list. Considering that it was ninety degrees out, four men in heavy, dark sweatshirts were bound to attract attention. Might even be the reason the armored-car guard drew on them first when he was coming out the drugstore. That and the fact that all of them were tooled up. Course, if Antonius and his boys hadn't smoked all that tree before the job, they might have thought the sweatshirts through. The sweatshirts, and the vanity plates on the getaway car. The plates were high up on that list too.

Antonius, braids touching his shoulders, sat back in his chair and maintained eye contact with the investigator seated across the table. Antonius was in the number one seat in the interview room, the inmate's spot, his back to a cream-colored wall. As he was currently housed in solitary, his legs were manacled. Other inmates were in various glassed-in rooms around them, talking to their lawyers, their girlfriends, their mothers, their wives. A guard sat in a nearby office, watching them. An alarm button had been mounted by the door of every room in the event that guard intervention was needed. Conversations here sometimes got amped.

"You musta been hot out in that parking lot," said the investigator, whose name was Phil Ornazian.

Antonius looked him over. Broad-shouldered dude with short black hair and a three-day beard flecked with gray. Late thirties, early forties. Wedding band on his ring finger. Almost looked like an Arab, with his prominent nose and large brown eyes. Antonius had assumed he was Muslim when they'd first met, but Ornazian was some brand of Christian. He'd mentioned once that he and his family attended an "apostolic" church. Whatever that was.

"You think?" said Antonius. "It was August in the District."

"The sweatshirts…whose idea was that?"

"Whose idea?"

"On the surveillance video, you guys are all standing around in winter clothing in the parking lot of the drugstore, and people are walking in and out of the store in T-shirts, polo shirts, and shorts. So I was just wondering, I was *curious,* who thought that was a good idea?"

It was Antonius's lifelong friend DeAndre who had insisted they wear the black sweatshirts in the middle of a Washington summer. Hoods up, so their faces wouldn't be caught on the cameras that were mounted on the building. DeAndre, that dumbass, never did do anything right. Boy could fuck up a birthday party at the Chuck E. Cheese.

"I don't recall," said Antonius.

Antonius was not trying to be difficult. He knew that Ornazian was there to assist him. The defense strategy was to paint DeAndre as the leader and decision maker of the group. To take that information into court and pull some of the shade off of Antonius. Ornazian was working for Antonius's lawyer, Matthew Mirapaul, trying to dig up dirt that would help him when he went to trial. But Antonius wasn't going to give up too many details about his boys, any of them, even though DeAndre had already put Antonius and the others in for the robbery. He had a code.

"Okay," said Ornazian. "Let's talk about your girlfriend."

"Sherry."

"You say you were with her at the time of the robbery."

"We were riding in my car together. She had called me to come pick her up over at the Giant off Rhode Island Avenue, in Northeast. Sherry had just bought a rack of groceries. She phoned me at, like, two in the afternoon, and I went over there to snatch her up. I got her at, like, two thirty."

"Why was she shopping at a Giant in Northeast when there's two Safeways in your neighborhood?"

"She likes that Giant."

"Anybody see you two together?"

"Nah. Not that I know. But, see, if the robbery was at three, and I was with her at two thirty, ain't no way I could get across town to Georgia Avenue, in Northwest, in time to be involved in what went down over there. All you got to do is pull up the phone records and you'll see that she called me at two. It proves that I wasn't there."

Ornazian made no comment. The phone call, of course, proved nothing of the kind. Sherry, the girlfriend, most likely *had* made the call, as she had been instructed to do. That, too, had been part of the plan. It was weed logic, creating an alibi through a phone call without a third-party eyewitness to corroborate the event. Unfortunately, there was no one who could testify and put Antonius and Sherry together at the time of the robbery.

Along with his own investigation, the prosecution's discovery, and the store's surveillance-camera footage, this is what Ornazian knew: Nearly two years earlier, on a sweltering midsummer day, an armed security guard had collected the daily cash deposits from a Rite Aid on upper Georgia Avenue and was in the process of exiting the building with canvas bags in hand. He was on the way to the company's armored truck idling out front.

Waiting in the parking lot were four men in their early twenties, wearing black sweatshirts, hoods up, and sweating profusely. All were armed with semiautomatic handguns. The driver of the armored car could have seen one of them in his side mirror, but he was not paying attention, as, counter to company policy, he was eating the lunch he had recently purchased from the KFC / Taco Bell up near the District line.

The men in the parking lot were Antonius Roberts, DeAndre Watkins, Rico Evans, and Mike Young. They mostly spent their time in the basement of Antonius's grandmother, who owned a house in Manor Park, where Antonius had a bed. There they smoked copious amounts of marijuana, watched conspiracy-theory documentaries on television, played video games, and made poorly produced rap videos and occasionally videos of themselves engaging in boxing and mixed martial arts matches, though none of them had studied or trained.

One afternoon someone got the idea to go over to the local drugstore on Georgia and observe the details of the daily cash pickup. They did this, stoned as Death Row rappers, for several days straight. It was always the same roly-poly dude came out with the bags, didn't look like he'd put up any kind of fight, didn't look like he could run or jump one foot off the ground. If you drew on him, said DeAndre, what could he do?

The guard's name was Yohance Brown, and he was not as passive or as physically incapable as he appeared to be. Brown was ex-military and had done two combat-heavy tours of Iraq. Though he had put on weight after his return to the States, Brown took no man's shit.

The day of the attempted robbery, the four accomplices arrived in two cars.

As Yohance Brown entered the protected entranceway of the drugstore, walled by sliding automatic glass doors front and back, he saw the hooded robbers standing in the parking lot, spaced out like gunmen in an Italian Western, holding nine-millimeter pistols tight against their thighs. As one of them raised his nine, Brown dropped the cash bags to the floor, pulled his Glock from its holster, calmly steadied his gun hand, and commenced firing. The robbers ran toward their cars, shooting over their shoulders in the direction of the store. Later, a flattened slug was found inside a Twinkie in the Rite Aid. Miraculously, no customers had been injured.

One of the robbers, Mike Young, was shot in the back by Brown. Young was later dropped off like dirty laundry outside the ER doors of Washington Hospital Center by Rico Evans, the driver of a Hyundai sedan day-rented from a Park View resident. Young survived.

Antonius and DeAndre got into an old Toyota Corolla, owned by DeAndre's cousin Rhonda, and sped north on

Georgia Avenue. Traffic cameras recorded the Corolla's vanity plates, which read ALIZE, the brand name of a cognac-based liqueur popular in certain quadrants of the city. Later, at the Fourth District police station, officers of various races and ethnicities watched the traffic-camera footage repeatedly, laughing their asses off at the idiots who had driven a vanity-plated car to an armed robbery, laughing even harder at the word *Alize*. By then all the suspects had been apprehended and arrested. DeAndre Watkins quickly flipped on his friends in exchange for reduced charges. He was currently on the fourth floor of the Correctional Treatment Facility, the hot block most commonly referred to by inmates as "the snitch hive."

"How's Sherry doing?" said Ornazian.

"She's a little agitated at me right now," said Antonius. "See, I was using the phone here in the jail, called this *other* girl I know. I needed someone new, Phil. I been with Sherry a long time, and I can't get sprung by the same-old. *You* know how that is."

"So, you had phone sex with this girl who wasn't your girl-friend."

"Uh-huh."

"I told you before, the jailhouse phones are bugged."

"Yeah, well, you were right. The Feds recorded my conversation with this girl, then played the tape back for Sherry to make her angry. They trying to get her to testify against me, say I was in on the robbery."

"And?"

"Sherry was madder than a mad dog," said Antonius. "But, see, that's my girl right there. She'll stand tall."

Antonius was a man with needs, maybe more than most.

8

He was good-looking and charismatic, which hurt him more than helped him. He was currently housed in the solitary-confinement unit known as South 1. He was being punished for having sexual relations with a female guard. Inmates claimed there were only two spots in the D.C. Jail that were safe for sex or shankings, out of view of cameras. Antonius thought he had found one of the spots. He had been mistaken.

Ornazian fired up his laptop, set it on the table between them, found what he was looking for on YouTube, clicked on it, and turned the laptop around so that Antonius could see the screen. A video commenced to play. It featured Antonius, DeAndre, and several of their friends smoking blunts, boxing clumsily with their shirts off, and brandishing bottles of champagne and cognac as well as various firearms, including an AK-47. All of it set to a third-rate rap tune that they had freestyled themselves. Antonius couldn't help but smile a little. He was feeling nostalgic for the camaraderie of his friends and a time when he was free.

"The prosecutors are going to play this for the jury," said Ornazian.

"What's that got to do with the robbery?"

"Nothing."

"They just trying to assassinate my character."

"Correct."

Antonius shook his head ruefully. "Everybody be steppin on my dick."

Antonius's prospects were not good. He'd been in the jail awaiting trial for the past twenty-three months. The evidence against him was overwhelming. He was looking at twelve years in a federal joint. Lorton, the local prison over the river, had closed long ago, so he was going somewhere far away.

"How are you handling the hole?" said Ornazian.

"I don't mind it," said Antonius. "I got my own cell. Nobody bothers me down there. No situations, nothing like that."

"You getting out soon?"

"They supposed to move me back to Gen Pop any day."

"Let me ask you something. You ever come across a guy named Michael Hudson up on that unit?"

Antonius thought it over. "I know a dude goes by Hudson. Not really to speak to outside of a nod. Quiet, tall dude, keeps his hair close. Medium skin."

"Is he clean-shaven?" said Ornazian, road-testing Antonius's information.

"Nah, he wears a beard. Gets it full too. Heard he's in on a rip-and-run charge. He's waiting to go to trial."

"That's the guy," said Ornazian. "Could you pass on a message to him when you get out of solitary?"

"Sure," said Antonius. "What you want me to tell him?"

"Just tell him Phil Ornazian said, 'Everything is going to be fine.'"

"I got you."

"Thanks, Antonius. I'm sorry I couldn't do more for you."

"Wasn't your fault. You tried."

Ornazian reached across the table. He and Antonius bumped fists.

TWO

MEN IN orange jumpsuits stood in an orderly line, waiting patiently to talk to a woman who was seated at a desk bolted to the jailhouse floor. On the desk was a paper circulation log, a stack of DCPL book receipts, and a pen. Beside the desk was a rolling cart with shelves holding books. The cell doors of the General Population unit had been opened remotely by a guard in a glassed-in station that was known as "the fishbowl." Two other guards were stationed in the unit, observing the proceedings, bored and disengaged. There was no need for them to be on high alert. When the book lady was on the block, the atmosphere was calm.

The woman at the desk was the mobile librarian of the D.C. Jail. The men addressed her as Anna, or Miss Anna if they were raised a certain way. On the job she wore no makeup and dressed in utilitarian and nonprovocative clothing. Her skin was olive, her hair black, her eyes a light shade of green. She had recently turned thirty, was a swimmer and biker, and kept herself fit. In the facility, she used her maiden name, Kaplan. On the street, and on her driver's license, she went with her husband's surname, which was Byrne.

"How you doin today, Anna?" said Donnell, a rangy young guy with sleepy eyes.

"I'm good, Donnell. How are you?"

"Maintaining. You got that chapter-book I asked for?"

From the cart beside her, Anna found the novel Donnell had requested and put it in his hand. She entered his name, the title of the book, his inmate identification number, cell, and return date in the log.

"Can't nobody mess with Dave Robicheaux," said Donnell.

"I hear he's pretty indestructible," said Anna.

"Can I ask you something?"

"Sure."

"You got any books that, you know, explain women?"

"What do you mean, *explain* them?"

"I got this one girlfriend, man, I don't *know*. Like, I can't figure out what she thinking from day to day. Women can be, you know, mysterious. Sayin, is there a book you could recommend?"

"Like a manual?"

"Yeah."

"Maybe you should read a novel *written* by a woman. That might give you an idea of the kinds of things that go on in a woman's head."

"You got any recommendations?"

"Let me think on it. In the meantime, that Robicheaux is due in a week, when I come back."

"What if I don't finish it by then?"

"You can renew it for one more week."

"Okay, then. Cool."

Donnell walked away. The next inmate stepped up to the table.

"Lorton Legends," said the man, asking for a novel that was often requested but unavailable inside the walls. The book was set in the old prison and on D.C.'s streets. "You got that?"

"We don't," said Anna. "Didn't you ask for this same book last week?"

"Thought y'all might've got it in *since* then."

By policy, sexually explicit books and books that promoted violence were not available in the jail library. Some urban fiction made the cut, some did not. Certain heavily requested books that espoused outlandish conspiracy theories, like *Behold a Pale Horse* and *The Forty-Eight Laws of Power,* were also prohibited. The sexuality and violence standards set by the D.C. Public Library for the detention facility were murky and often went unenforced. Some serial-killer novels and soft-core potboilers made it through the gates. Anna had once seen a group of inmates in the dayroom watching a DVD of *The Purge.*

"What you got for me, then?" said the man. "Don't give me no boring stuff."

On the cart, Anna found something by Nora Roberts, a prolific, popular novelist who typically generated good feedback, and gave it to the man. She began to log the details of the inmate and the novel.

"I read one of hers before," said the man, inspecting the jacket. "She's cool. That'll work."

As he drifted, the next man came up to the table. He was tall, with a full beard and close-cut hair. Anna knew little about him except for his reading habits. He was nice-looking, had a lean build, and spoke with soft confidence. His name was Michael Hudson.

"Mr. Hudson."

"What do you have for me today, Miss Anna?"

She handed him two books that she had chosen for him when she had staged her cart the previous afternoon. One was a story collection called *Kentucky Straight.* The other was a single volume with two Elmore Leonard Western novels, written early in his career.

Inmates could check out two books a week. She often gave Michael longish books or volumes containing multiple novels because he tended to run through the material very quickly. In the past year, since he had first been incarcerated, he had become a voracious reader. His tastes ran to stories occurring outside of East Coast cities. He liked to read books about the kinds of people he'd not met growing up in Washington, set in places he'd never visited. Nothing too difficult or dense. He preferred stories that were clearly written and simply told. He read for entertainment. Michael was new to this. He wasn't trying to impress anyone. But his tastes were evolving. He was learning.

He studied the jackets, glanced at the inner flap of *Kentucky Straight.*

"The stories in that book are set mainly in Appalachia," said Anna.

"Like, mountain folk," said Michael.

"Uh-huh. The author grew up there. I think you'll like the Westerns too."

"Yeah, Leonard. That dude's real."

"You read *Swag.* One of his crime novels."

"I remember." Michael looked her in the eye. "Thank you, Miss Anna."

"Just doing my job."

"So, tell me a couple more titles. For later."

As Michael had gotten more into reading, he had asked Anna to recommend some books for him to read in the future, either upon his release or when he transitioned to prison. Novels that were not in her inventory or were deemed inappropriate for the inmates. Books she thought he might like. She gave him the titles verbally. He'd write them down later, tell them to his mother when she came to visit. His mother had been surprised, and pleased, that he had developed an interest in books.

"*Hard Rain Falling,*" she said. "By Don Carpenter. And a short-story collection called *The Things They Carried,* by Tim O'Brien. It's set in Vietnam, during the war."

"*Hard Rain Falling,* Carpenter," repeated Michael. "*Things They Carried.*"

"Tim O'Brien."

"Got it." He stood there, as if waiting.

The man behind him said, "*Shit.* My hair about to go gray."

"Is there something else?" said Anna.

"Just want to say…I never read a book in my life before I came in here. You know that, right? This pleasure I got now, it's because of you."

"The DCPL put a branch in here a couple of years ago. That's why you get to read books. But I'm glad you're taking advantage of the opportunity. I hope you like those."

"I'll let you know."

"You're coming to book club next week, right?"

"You *know* I am," said Michael.

"I'll see you in the chapel."

"Right."

She watched him walk toward his cell. He was rubbing the

cover of one of the books as if he were polishing something precious in his hands.

THERE WAS a law library in the detention facility that the inmates used to research their cases. Anna had worked there when she'd first come to the jail.

The law library was available to members of each housing unit for two hours per week and to inmates who were in Restricted Housing by request. A civilian law librarian ran the operation and was assisted by a legal clerk who was an inmate, a desirable, soft-labor position in the jail. Inmates had access to reading materials and to LexisNexis programs on computers but had no access to e-mail services or the internet. In addition to research, the law library's space was used for voting, which was available to non-felons only, and for SAT and GED testing.

Though the D.C. Jail's library was an official branch of the DCPL, it was not a traditional library in that inmates could not enter a room and browse through the stacks. An actual library was to open soon, but for now, books were delivered to the inmates on a cart.

There were fifteen units at the jail. The mobile librarian visited three units per day, so every unit received her services once a week. Among the units were GED, General Population, Fifty and Older, Mental Health, Juvenile, and Restricted Housing. Each unit had its own characteristics and needs. It was part of Anna's job to anticipate those needs when she staged her carts and chose titles from the over three thousand books housed in the workroom. The library stocked paperbacks only.

Four thirty was her quitting time. Anna was in the workroom and had been staging her cart for the Fifty and Older unit, which she was scheduled to visit the following morning. That particular unit housed mostly repeat offenders, parole violators, and drug addicts. She chose a couple of Gillian Flynn novels, popular among inmates, and some early Stephen Kings. Anything by King was in heavy play. The Harry Potter books were wildly popular as well.

Anna's assistant, Carmia, a recent graduate of UDC who had come up in public housing in Southeast, stood nearby, inspecting each book that had been returned, fanning through pages, checking for notes and contraband. For security reasons, books could not be passed from inmate to inmate. Each book was inspected between rentals.

"You almost ready, Anna?"

"Yes."

"We can walk out together. I got to get my boy out of day care."

"I'm nearly done."

Anna had been at the D.C. Jail for several years but not always in her current position. After her undergrad studies at Emerson, in Boston, she accompanied her husband, who had been hired as a junior attorney in a District law firm, to Washington, where she obtained her master's in library science at Catholic University. Her first job in town was as a law librarian in a firm on H Street. This bored her silly, so when she saw an ad posted by the Corrections Corporation of America for the position of law librarian of the D.C. Central Detention Facility, she applied. To her surprise, she was quickly hired.

Running the law library of the jail was her first encounter

with lockup. Initially, the experience was troubling, especially the daily security process and the ominous finality of doors closing, locks turning, and gates clanging shut. But these procedures and sounds soon became part of her routine, and quickly she found that she preferred dealing with inmates to dealing with attorneys. Interacting one-on-one with men who were incarcerated was not problematic. She was there to help them, and they knew it. It unsettled her, sometimes, to sit with a man charged with rape or pedophilia and direct him toward informational avenues of appeal. But she never felt threatened. Rather, she was unfulfilled. It wasn't a creative or particularly rewarding way to spend one's day. Also, she had a deep love of fiction, and she thought it would be cool to promote literature and literacy. So when the DCPL opened a library branch in the jail in the spring of 2015, she applied for the position of librarian and got the job.

"Coming?" said Carmia, a devout Christian with pretty brown eyes who was built small and stocky, like a low-to-the-ground running back.

Anna shut down her government cell phone, then gathered the few belongings she had brought into the jail and placed them in a clear plastic handbag.

"Let's go."

ANNA AND Carmia exited the D.C. Central Detention Facility and walked to the lot where they had parked their cars. They passed a variety of guards, visitors, administrators, and law enforcement officers, driving, headed on foot to their vehicles, or standing around, catching smokes and talking about their day. The jail was at Nineteenth and D, Southeast, on the eastern edge of the 20003 zip code and residential Kingman Park. Longtime natives knew the area mainly as the 190-acre Stadium-Armory Campus, which housed the jail, the former D.C. General Hospital, now an enormous homeless shelter, and the beloved RFK Stadium, where the Washington Redskins had played during their glory years.

"Have a blessed day," said Carmia, veering off toward a Japanese import that she would be paying on for the next five years.

"You also," said Anna. She found her car, a boxy black-over-cream Mercury Mariner, the discontinued sister car to the Ford Escape. It had good sight lines and fulfilled its function as an urban runner. More important to Anna, it was paid for.

Seagulls glided down from overhead and landed in a small group in the parking lot. It sometimes took her aback to see the birds but of course she was steps from the Anacostia River and not far from the Potomac and the Chesapeake Bay.

She got into her SUV and retrieved her wallet and personal cell from the glove box, where she locked them up each morning. She let down her hair and lowered her driver's-side window. Anna took a moment, breathed in fresh air, and listened to the call of the gulls.

THREE

PHIL ORNAZIAN stepped out of his house, a neat brick brownstone southeast of Grant Circle, in Petworth, on the 400 block of Taylor Street, Northwest. The closing of his front door muffled the sounds of his two raucous dogs, his laughing sons, and his wife, Sydney, who was chastising the boys for something, like trampolining on the furniture or throwing a ball in the living room, or…something. For being kids. They were doing what children do, and she was doing what mothers do. His role, as he conveniently saw it, was to keep the roof over their heads, the utilities on, and the refrigerator and pantry full. "Going hunting," he would typically say before he left the house. "Gotta drag the meat back to the cave." This was his unsubtle rationalization for the time he spent away from home.

Ornazian quickstepped off the porch, went down to the street, and opened the gate on the chain-link fence he'd had installed as soon as his older boy had learned to walk. Toys, balls, a trike, and a training-wheeled bike were in the "yard," which was mostly dirt. Ornazian couldn't get to his car, a 2013 double-black Ford Edge, fast enough.

Men like him were at peace only when they were away from home. The office, which for him was mostly his car and the streets, was much more orderly and controllable than his house. He was into his wife and his children but felt it was unnatural and unproductive for a man to work at home.

They had agreed early on that Sydney would raise the children and he would bring in the dosh. Syd did not have a paying job but she worked as hard as any person he knew. She was not insecure around women who were professionals and didn't want to miss out on the experience of being with her children as much as possible, knowing instinctively that time spent away from them, in a window that was, after all, very short, was time she could never get back. Unfortunately, it meant that they sacrificed extras and sometimes struggled financially. But Phil Ornazian was above all a hustler. When his legit business was not flourishing, when his investigation work dried up, as it tended to do, he improvised.

"Hello, Miss Mattie," he said, to an elderly neighbor who was walking her small, short-haired mutt whose coat had gone gray. They both moved very slowly.

"Phillip," she said. "Off to work?"

"Yes, ma'am."

Mattie Alston was one of the dwindling number of long-term home owners still on this block. Many of the homes had been sold off by their original owners at a tremendous profit or passed on to heirs who had either moved in themselves or taken the money and bought elsewhere. That was the upside of gentrification. Longtime property owners did well, if they wanted to. Renters, however, were typically displaced and left with nothing.

Ornazian had bought this house on the cheap when he was single, fifteen years earlier, before Petworth turned, before young, new-Camelot college graduates flowed in and put down roots in sections of the city that white Washingtonians had once fled. If he were to sell his house now, he'd walk with three, four hundred thousand dollars or more. But where would he go?

Ornazian got into his Ford, hit the push-button ignition, and heard the engine roar to life. With twenty-twos, custom rims, and extended pipes, the Sport model had a little more flair than the standard Edge, and it was as horsed up as a Mustang GT. Ornazian was something of a car freak and felt he needed the extra power in case he had to get out of trouble. That was how he explained it to his wife. Like all of the vehicles he had purchased since his marriage, this one was a wolf in sheep's clothing.

"What's this, then?" said Sydney, with her working-class-Brit accent, the day he'd driven the car home. From their concrete-and-brick-pillar porch, she eyed him and the black SUV suspiciously.

"Family car," said Ornazian.

"The Dale Earnhardt Jr. family," she'd said.

Ornazian took Fifth Street south to Park Place, going along the Soldiers' Home, and then back on Fifth, between the McMillan Reservoir and behind Howard University, bypassing the congestion of Georgia Avenue and coming out around Florida to the western edge of LeDroit Park. He was headed for New York Avenue and a quick route out of the city. Ornazian knew the backstreets and the shortcuts. He didn't need Waze or any other app. He'd lived in the District his whole life.

* * *

AT DUSK, he came off 295 onto Eastern Avenue, drove along the easternmost border of Maryland and D.C., crossed Minnesota Avenue, then hung a left and dipped off into Maryland.

A half mile out of the city, on a tough stretch of road, in a low-income area of Prince George's County, he parked in a lot before a complex of brick buildings, a one-stop-shop arrangement catering to various needs. There was a barbecue restaurant with a drive-through, a supper club touting dancers, a barbershop, a pawnbroker, a check-cashing service, and a liquor store with barred windows. Beside the liquor store were the offices of a bail bondsman. The sign outside read WARD BONDS, 24 HOURS, AT YOUR SERVICE. A phone number was prominently displayed below the words.

At the door of Ward Bonds, Ornazian rang a buzzer, looked up into a camera mounted on the brick wall, and heard a click. He stepped into a kind of lobby, a small waiting area bordered by a dirty wall of Plexiglas, through which it was just possible to make out the main office. Customers or potential clients could talk to the employees through a circle of holes bored through the Plexiglas until they were cleared for entry. The setup resembled a combination bank and urban Chinese carryout.

There was a door at the end of the Plexiglas wall and again someone buzzed him through. He walked past scattered desks, mostly empty, three of them occupied by two men and one woman, all in their twenties, wearing company T-shirts and Dickies slacks. One of the men nodded at Ornazian as he continued on to a glassed-in office. There behind a desk sat Thaddeus Ward, late sixties, barrel-chested, and hard to hurt. He was snaggletoothed and sported a neat gray mustache.

Ward stood, came to Ornazian with a brisk, square-shouldered step, and shook his hand.

"Been a while," said Ward. "You could visit."

"It's not like I'm out here too often. When you had your offices in D.C., I saw you more."

"Ain't no bail-bond business in D.C. anymore. Only skips. Criminals got that nonfinancial-release option there. I *had* to come out to P.G."

"I know it."

"You only come by when you need something," said Ward.

"Didn't realize you were so sensitive, Thaddeus. You want a hug or something?"

"If I wanted to touch you, I'd bend you over my desk."

"Don't be so butch."

"Glad you called me, though. I could use a little extra. Got too many people on my payroll right now and not enough work."

"Then lay some of them off."

"Can't do that. They're veterans."

"See? You *are* sensitive."

"*Fuck* you, man." Ward went back behind his desk. "Let me just call Sharon and tell her I'll be out tonight."

As Ward picked up his cell and speed-dialed his daughter, Ornazian examined a wall where many cheaply framed photographs hung. There were several of Ward and his buddies, standing and seated around their hooches in the Central Highlands of Vietnam. They looked like kids, and many were. Ward himself had told a lie and enlisted when he was seventeen years old. In another photo, Ward cradled an M-60 machine gun and posed next to a photographic collage of topless women, images cut from magazines and glued to a large piece of cardboard. Other photographs showed Ward in his Metropolitan Police Department uniform, in plainclothes, accepting commendations from a senior officer in a white shirt. Ward shaking hands with Jesse Jackson. Ward with Darrell Green. Art Monk. And one incongruous photograph of a champion heavyweight boxer standing next to a nearly identical younger man who had to be his son. The boxer was wearing the champ belt over his suit pants. The son, also a former boxer but with an undistinguished career in the ring, had his hand on his father's shoulder.

Ward had finished his call and came up on Ornazian.

"What's up with that?" said Ornazian, nodding at the father-and-son photo.

"When I was working Vice, long time ago, I busted this massage parlor on Fourteenth and R. Found this photograph, a glossy signed to the establishment by the champ's son. Not to cast aspersions…"

"You've got it hanging on your wall of fame. It must mean something to you."

"It just makes me smile," said Ward. "But really, it reminds me of those Wild West times. I drove down Fourteenth Street recently. You know what that massage-parlor building is now? A flower store."

"So? That's a good thing, right?"

"Sure, a positive thing. But when it was wide open out there, we had fun. There was this other dude, back in the seventies, was a real gunslinger. Street name was Red Fury. Had a girl-friend named Coco, a pimpette who ran a whorehouse on that same stretch of Fourteenth. You heard of Red?"

"Before my time."

"I could tell you some things."

"We're going to be spending hours together tonight. Tell me then."

They walked to the outer office, where Ward introduced Ornazian to the three employees who were seated at their desks. None of them looked very busy now. One of the men, Jake, stacked shoulders and neck, barely made eye contact with Ornazian. The other, who said his name was Esteban, was courteous and shook Ornazian's hand firmly. The woman, Genesis, had the most intelligent, alert eyes of the group. She wore a ball cap and a ring with a very small diamond on her finger.

"Just one a' y'all mind the phones tonight," said Ward. "Don't care who. Decide amongst yourselves. I'll be checking in."

By the time they exited the offices, night had fallen. Behind the building, Ward kept three black cars: two Lincoln Marks and an old but cherry Crown Victoria. Ward had expanded his business beyond bail bonds and skip traces. He now provided security for events and drivers/bodyguards for celebrities, dignitaries, and quasi-celebrities who came into D.C.

As they walked toward the cars, Ornazian said, "What's the quiet one's story?"

"Jake did a combat tour in Iraq and re-upped for a second tour in Afghanistan. He's on so many meds I can't use him on the street. I keep him in the office to answer the phones and process clients. He's a house cat."

"What about the other dude?"

"Esteban. That's Spanish for Stephen."

"No kidding."

"I'm just sayin. Marine Corps. Follows orders real good and aims to please."

"And the woman?"

"National Guard, but don't let that fool you. She ran security with convoys. Went into hot pockets when the soldiers and Marines got pinned down. I talked to her CO and he told me that girl was fierce. But I won't have her for long. Genesis is finishing college on the VA tit. Wants to go to law school."

"Good for her."

"What I should have done, too, if I had any sense. But I didn't. Not a lick." Ward pointed to the Crown Vic. "Let's take my UC. It's all loaded up."

As they cruised out of the lot, Ward nodded at his sign. "Changed the name of my business, you notice that? Used to be Ward Bail Bonds, but now it's just Ward Bonds. It's clever, don't you think?"

"Why is it clever?"

"Ward Bond. The actor?"

"Not familiar with him. Is he from the silent era or something?"

"Funny. He's that big dude, character actor. Played in all of them movies with John Wayne."

"I've heard of *Lil* Wayne," said Ornazian.

"Now you're being stupid," said Ward.

FOR YEARS, several hotels and motels had been clustered around the busy intersection of New York Avenue and

Bladensburg Road near the National Arboretum and the city's largest animal shelter. These establishments had been homes to folks on public assistance, drug addicts, thrifty adulterers, down-and-outers, death-wish drinkers, and unknowing foreign tourists who had purchased cheap lodging online that promised easy bus access to the monuments, museums, and downtown D.C. The motels had also been notorious venues for prostitutes and pimps, but that activity had been curtailed. The rooms were now mostly occupied by homeless families who had been placed here by the District government. Private, armed security guards roamed the parking lots, keeping an eye on the comings and goings of the residents.

Adjoining one of the motels was a Chinese restaurant with a large dining room. Its grim location and lack of ambience prevented it from becoming a destination for discerning Washingtonians, but it was a secret spot for foodies who didn't mind the traffic congestion and the enduring blight of the NYA corridor.

Ornazian and Ward sat at a four-top, eating and strategizing. The proprietors specialized in Szechuan cooking of the northern Shaanxi region. The food was righteous.

"Pass me those scallion pancakes, man," said Ward.

Ornazian pushed the plate within reaching distance of Ward. Also on the table were platters with dwindling portions of *rou jia mo*, which was the Chinese version of a hamburger, cumin lamb on sticks, spicy vermicelli, and dumplings with hot sauce. They were having a feast.

Ward swallowed, closing his eyes with satisfaction. "You trying to spoil a brother."

"Maybe."

He opened his eyes. "You bring me over to these hotels cause of the location? Like, a prelude?"

"I brought you to this restaurant because of the food. Anyway, you'd be hard pressed to find pimps around here now."

"True," said Ward, somewhat ruefully. "The game changed. Most of the trade is online these days."

"Get on certain internet sites, you pick out your girl. Then it's an in-call or an out-call. You don't have to troll the streets looking for it. It's as easy as making a dinner reservation."

"Police have been stinging the johns like that, though. Luring them to hotels with net ads."

"They make some arrests that way, yeah. But they haven't made a dent in prostitution."

"I remember when all those Asian massage parlors were in D.C."

"Police in the District did a good job of going after the landlords. They pretty much closed the massage parlors down. Most of the AMPs are over in Northern Virginia now." Ornazian stabbed at a dumpling and moved it to his plate. "Hispanics have the brothels. That leaves the street trade. Logan Circle is still a hot spot, but less of one. The girls work the clubs early in the night and then move over to the hotels. Near dawn you still see some trickin on the corners. But it's not like it was."

"Lot of those online ads say 'No pimps.'"

"Lotta those ads are bullshit," said Ornazian. "There's still plenty of pimps around. The ads say 'No pimps' so the johns don't get scared away."

"Tell me about the one you got in mind."

"We'll get to that. Let's enjoy our meal. Get another dish. Try the black bean eggplant if you want to go to heaven."

"I would, but our waiter don't understand a word of English. Kinda hard to communicate in this joint."

"You ever try to learn Chinese?"

"Why would I?"

"Just point to the photograph on the menu. That's what the pics are for."

"I shouldn't eat any more. But okay."

Ward raised his hand and tried to get the waiter's attention. Ornazian texted his wife and suggested she go to sleep. He told her he'd see her in the morning.

FOUR

THEY DROVE out to the old residential section of Beltsville, in Maryland, and parked in a neighborhood of ramshackle, trailer-type homes on a street between Route 1 and Rhode Island Avenue. There was little activity on the block, though there were many cars and trucks, three or four to a home. Some were in mid-repair; some had been left in weeds for seasons, perhaps years. Ornazian and Ward were near a government strip of land that served as a walk-through between blocks. Like the rest of the surroundings, this too had gone untended. Trees had fallen, blocking the path.

"That's his," said Ornazian, nodding toward a house on the edge of the walk-through.

"With the portable carport?" said Ward. "That's some ghetto shit right there. In a different hood, the neighbors would call the county on this mug."

The house was a one-story affair with a side addition fronted in the formstone commonly found on dwellings in Baltimore. The original structure had asbestos shingles and a few of them had fallen off, exposing tar paper. The carport was just a corrugated cover on four poles that sat free in the driveway. There was no vehicle beneath it.

"The pimps I knew in my day had more pride," said Ward. "I mean, they never *did* have much money. Spent most of it on their rides and their vines. It was all about the show."

"It's smarter *not* to show."

"How'd you mark him?"

"I talked to a girl, goes by the name of Monique. Did her a solid once. Regular john she had had stiffed her out some money. She'd been busted a couple of times for solicitation, and she'd seen me down at the courts."

"You found the john."

"Wasn't hard. She was making out-calls to this guy, always used the same hotel, one of those new boutique jobs, down near the White House? Guy always valeted his car. I slipped one of the valet dudes some cash in exchange for the plate number. From there I found his home address. Married with kids, naturally. He's the CFO of some tech company out on Twenty-Nine."

"You blackmailed him," said Ward.

"He shouldn't have stiffed my friend."

"So this girl, Monique, she hipped you to this pimp."

"I asked her what was happening out there. You were a cop, so you know that prostitutes are the best sources on the street. They're up all night. They see everything."

"Indeed."

"Monique told me about this pimp she had for a while. Goes by Theodore."

"That's not a very cool name for a player."

"But it is," said Ornazian, who was a hobbyist in the origin of words. "It's from the Greek. *Theo* is 'god,' and *doro* is 'gift.' God's gift. Get it?"

"You some kind of linguist?"

Ornazian grinned. "I'm a cunning linguist."

"Finish your story, man."

"Theodore's got a stable, three women at all times. If they want to leave him or if they don't earn, he lets them go. His philosophy is, there's plenty more where they came from. He's no gorilla pimp. He's not into violence. He likes to smoke weed, and so do they, but it's not part of his plan to make them dependent on harder drugs. He looks for girls who have problems, like problems at home, with their parents, all that. He listens to them. He makes them his girlfriends. Buys them gifts. Puts them up in a decent place. And then, he's like, 'All these good things cost money. You gonna need to *contribute*, girl. Take care of my man here and help me out. And this man right here.' Like that. He holds the money they earn. They don't keep any of it, but he takes care of all their needs."

"Theodore," said Ward.

Ward had said the name with hate. It was one of the many reasons Ornazian had asked Ward to come along tonight.

"Take a nap," said Ornazian. "He's not coming home for another hour or so."

"How you know?"

"I been out here three nights this week. Man's a creature of habit, just like anyone else."

"I mean, how you know what he's got?"

"He's working three women. Monique says they each earn about a thousand a night on the weekends. Put that together with what he probably keeps in the house, and it could be a

33

nice payday. The dude makes a couple hundred thousand a year, cash. Chances are some of it's in his crib."

"We gonna hit him before he goes in?"

"No. That window on the right side of the house, closest to us? That's the bathroom. Every night, he comes home, the light goes on in there and then the window steams up."

"I get it. The man likes to shower before he retires."

Ornazian settled into his seat. "Take a nap, Thaddeus."

"I gotta pee."

"There's an empty milk jug behind your seat."

"I can't if you're watching."

"I'll turn away."

Ward side-glanced Ornazian. "Could you tug on it a little?"

"Only if that will shut you up."

AROUND THREE in the morning, Theodore drove his Chrysler 300 under the cut-rate carport and killed the engine. He got out of his black Green Hornet–style sedan and walked toward his house. He was tall and very thin and wore his hair in braids. He sported a down vest over a red buffalo-check shirt, jeans with appliques on the pockets, and Timbs.

"Don't look like a mack to me," said Ward.

"That's today's pimp," said Ornazian. "You know where you find guys wearing outrageous clothes, carrying walking sticks, and shit like that? At Halloween and frat parties."

Theodore triggered a motion-detector light as he stepped up to his door.

"He got those security lights around back too?"

"Yeah," said Ornazian. "So what? His house backs up to woods. Anyway, we're gonna be inside quick."

"Are there dogs?"

"No dogs."

"I hate fuckin with dogs."

"I crept around that house many times. He has no dogs. Trust me." As Theodore entered his house and closed the door behind him, Ornazian said, "Okay."

Ward had disabled the dome light of the Vic. They exited in darkness and went around to the rear of the car, where Ward popped the trunk. He fired up a mini Maglite he had produced from his jacket and put the butt end of it in his mouth, illuminating the trunk's interior.

In the trunk was a great deal of weaponry, ammunition, and hardware, as well as various restraint devices. From a box, Ornazian and Ward pulled lightly powdered nitrile gloves, favored by auto mechanics, and fitted them on their hands. Ward unrolled a blanketed 12-gauge Remington pump-action shotgun, then lifted a Glock nine out of a case. He released its magazine, checked the load, and seated the magazine back into the gun. The Remington 870 and the Glock 17 were common police firearms. Ward fitted the pistol into the dip of his slacks.

"The Special's you," said Ward, nodding at a .38 revolver that was a version of the MPD sidearm Ward had carried when he was first in uniform.

"You know I don't want it," said Ornazian.

"It's for show," said Ward.

Ornazian broke the cylinder on the .38 and saw that its chambers were loaded. He slipped the gun in the side pocket of his lightweight jacket, then grabbed a friction-lock, retractable baton from a large steel toolbox and put it in a back pocket of his jeans. Ward handed Ornazian a package of women's stockings. Ornazian pulled a stocking down over his face and Ward did the same. Finally, Ward put some plastic cuffs of varying lengths in his jacket, picked up the shotgun, cradled it, and shut the trunk. He nodded at Ornazian.

They moved to the side of the house, watched through windows as its interior brightened, waited for the bathroom light to come on, and stood outside its window for several minutes until they heard the sigh of pipes followed by the faint drum of water running in a shower. Ward followed Ornazian to the backyard. A security light flooded the area and Ornazian stepped into it, unfazed. He calmly used the steel baton to break the window of a rear door. He reached inside the broken window, unlocked the knob, and flipped the arm of the dead bolt.

They entered the house and walked through an odorous kitchen to a living area with a wide-screen television, a table holding game-console controllers and stroke magazines, and a matching set of large leather furniture. The house was rank with crushed-out cigarettes and the skunk-smell of weed.

Down a hall were a couple of bedrooms and, at the end, a bathroom door. Behind it, Theodore showered. Ornazian scouted the bedrooms while Ward stood in the hall, the shotgun resting on his forearm.

Ornazian found the bedroom where Theodore obviously slept and switched on the bedside lamp. The nightstand's top drawer had a keyhole on its face. A smartphone, presently charging in a wall outlet, was on the nearby dresser. There was a wooden chair on which Theodore most likely sat when he put on his socks and shoes. An open closet showed many shirts, top-buttoned and neatly hung on a wooden rod. On the carpet of the closet, Nike sneaks and Timberland and Nike boots were paired, neatly aligned, and set atop their corresponding boxes.

Soon the sound of running water ceased. Ward, positioned outside the bathroom, pointed the shotgun at the door, fitting its butt in the crook of his shoulder, his finger inside the trigger guard. Theodore stepped out of the bathroom, still wet, wearing only a bath towel around his waist.

"Fuck is this," he said, getting a look at the man before him holding the shotgun dead-on at his chest.

Ward racked the pump for drama. "You don't know?"

"You fixin to rob me," said Theodore. It wasn't a question. He was trying to remain cool but his face had lost some color.

"Correct," said Ward, jerking his head toward the bedroom on the left. "In there."

Theodore walked into the bedroom and Ward followed. Ornazian had drawn the .38 and was holding it by his side.

"Drop that towel," said Ward. Theodore did not comply and Ward said, "Drop it."

Theodore pulled the towel free and dropped it to the floor. He stood naked before the men who held the guns. He was bird-chested and inadequately muscled.

"For a man who runs women," said Ward, "you don't look like much."

In truth, there was nothing wrong with Theodore. He was all there, more or less. But Ward knew that a naked man was a vulnerable man. He was simply stripping him down further.

"Sit on that chair," said Ward. To Ornazian he said, "Cover him."

Theodore took a seat on the wooden chair. Ward placed the shotgun on the bed as Ornazian pointed the pistol at Theodore. Ward used the plastic cuffs to bind Theodore's wrists in front of him and the longer ties to secure his ankles to the legs of the chair.

Ward looked at Ornazian, whose eyes said, *Go ahead*. They had discussed the plan in the Crown Vic. Ward had interrogated prisoners in Nam, and he had questioned countless suspects in police stations all over the District with, one could assume, often unorthodox tactics. Ward had experience. Ornazian was happy to let him lead.

"I see you got a lock on that nightstand," said Ward. "Where the key at?"

"In the drawer below it," said Theodore.

"Course it is," said Ward. He knew that everyone, straights and criminals alike, kept their money and valuables in their bedrooms, close by, within reach.

Ward opened the lower drawer, saw condoms, lubrication, loose change, and a key wrapped up in a piece of tissue paper. He used the key to unlock the upper drawer. Inside that drawer was a semiauto Beretta, an extra magazine, and rubber-banded stacks of cash. Ward pocketed the gun and the magazine, fanned through the cash, and tossed the stacks on the bed.

"Where's the rest of your money?" said Ward.

"That's all of it," said Theodore, staring straight ahead.

Ward went to the closet, pulled the shirts aside, and looked behind them. Then he got down to floor level and checked the shoeboxes. All matched up except for a fresh pair of Jordans sitting atop a box with the brand name Stacy Adams. Ward pulled this box out from under the sneakers and looked inside. More money. Stacks of it.

"You tryin to bankrupt a man," said Theodore.

"Is that all of it?"

"You cleaned me out."

"All the money you make, and this is it?"

"I got overhead," said Theodore.

"The pimp's lament," said Ward.

Ward took the money off the bed and put it together with the money in the Stacy Adams box. He went to the dresser, unplugged the iPhone from its charger, and dropped the phone in Theodore's lap. It slipped off his thigh and fell to the floor.

"After we leave," said Ward, "you can figure out a way to pick up your phone and hit up one of your girls or whoever. You got a toolbox somewhere in this mess. Won't be hard for someone to cut you free."

"I ain't gonna forget this."

"Don't speak. Let me tell you how it's gonna be." Ward handed the shoebox to Ornazian and picked up the shotgun. "You *will* forget it. What you need to do now is, you got to put a Band-Aid on your pride and move on. 'Cause if you try to find out who we are, if you ask your neighbors if they seen a car out front tonight, anything like that…if I go down in any way, if I get locked up, even if I die of natural causes? Someone gonna step out the shadows one night and murder your ass. Do you understand me, Theodore?"

"I understand that you messed with the wrong man."

"Thought I told you: not another word."

"Fuck you, old man."

Ward reversed his grip on the shotgun and swung its stock. Ornazian looked away.

THEY DROVE south on Route 1, stopped at an IHOP in College Park, and had breakfast among nightcrawlers and University of Maryland students eating off their highs and drunks. Back out in the car, Ornazian counted out the money below the sight line of the dash.

"Eight thousand each, give or take," said Ornazian, handing the shoebox to Ward. "After my expenses. I'm going to give a thousand dollars to Monique."

"What else you gonna give her?"

"Say what?"

"You tappin that ass?"

Ornazian shook his head. "I'm spoken for."

"Mr. True Blue," said Ward. "Call me if you got something else. That was easy money right there."

"It's four mortgage payments," said Ornazian. "That's what this is about for me."

"That's not all it is. You like it. You 'specially like when we out here saving someone. Like that woman and her kids got kidnapped by that crew on Kennedy Street? You were *all* fired up on that one."

"So were you."

"Least I admit it," said Ward.

"It was a job."

"Nah, Phil. I knew dudes like you in the Nam. Had that hero thing goin on. Couldn't keep their heads down, even though

40

they knew better. Had to run to the action. Not for nothing, some of those guys didn't come back."

"That's not me."

"No?"

"I'm just trying to take care of my family."

"You didn't enjoy it tonight?"

"Not like you."

"You talking about Theodore? You think I liked that?"

"A little," said Ornazian.

"It was about respect. I told him not to run his gums. Boy couldn't help hisself."

Ward ignitioned the car. They drove back into Northeast, saying nothing further, the silence between them not uncomfortable in the least, as it is for certain kinds of men. Ornazian was thinking of his wife and children. Ward had planned a dinner with his daughter for later that day. He'd order food in. Maybe they would watch a game on TV.

FIVE

THE BOOK club was held in the jail's chapel and available to the Gen Pop and Fifty and Older units. The first ten inmates to sign up for the club were admitted. The session ran for sixty to ninety minutes and was always full. Even if the attendees were not particularly book lovers, the session filled up quickly, as it was something to break the numbing routine of incarceration. Once a book was assigned, the inmates had three weeks to read it before the discussion. The meetings were led by Anna, the jailhouse librarian.

Anna provided a reader's guide to the attendees complete with questions, similar to the guides found in the back of some trade paperbacks. The guide was just an aid to help them think about what they were reading and how to discuss it. When she passed out the guides she stressed that answering the questions was optional. She meant for the club to be enjoyable. The last thing she wanted to do was give them homework.

The chapel was not ornate but it was low lit and a quiet place to meditate, away from the cell blocks and common rooms. There was a lectern and chairs, and audiovisual equipment could be brought in if needed. A local nonprofit, the Free Minds Book Club, ran a reading and writing program in the chapel for incarcerated juveniles who had been charged as adults and were waiting to transition into the federal prison system. The juvenile inmates, who were housed in their own unit, read books, discussed them with visiting authors, and wrote essays and poems that were eventually published in a glossy magazine that was sold in coffee shops throughout the city. The group also produced a lively newsletter.

Anna's book club was less formal, did not involve writing, and was strictly a program to promote an appreciation of reading. She had no illusions that she was positively affecting the inmates' lives as a group. But she wasn't sure that she was failing to do that either. She hoped to reach someone. Maybe *just* one. Like many teachers and counselors, all she could do was try to pull someone through the keyhole in the end.

She had chosen *Of Mice and Men* for this group of inmates, who were housed in the Gen Pop unit. It was a linear tale, cleanly told, and, with its overt symbolism, easily taught. She knew there would be much to discuss. The novel was too short to sustain a three-week read, and subsequently many of the men had read it twice.

In picking the material, Anna had to remember that the inmates had varying degrees of education and intellect. A good many of them had not graduated high school. Most were inexperienced readers. Material that was difficult or dense could frustrate an inmate and permanently turn him off to reading. *The Heart Is a Lonely Hunter* had been notably unpopular. One inmate claimed that reading the McCullers novel had driven him to thoughts of suicide, and he was not entirely joking.

The men in orange jumpsuits sat in a circular arrangement of chairs, Anna a link in the circle. Among the group were Antonius Roberts, who had recently come out of the hole, Donnell, and Michael Hudson. The inmates held their paperback books in their hands or kept them on the floor beneath their chairs. Two armed guards were in the room in radio contact with additional security at all times, but the men in the book club were generally pleased to be there. Conflict was not on their minds.

"WE SHOULD start," said Anna.

"Let's have our minute," said an inmate named Larry who was up on felony manslaughter charges and had recently given himself over to God.

Most of them bowed their heads for a silent prayer. There were Muslims, a variety of Christians, some agnostics, and a few atheists in the room. Some closed their eyes, mouthed words, others just sat respectfully and waited out the silence. One of the guards said a personal prayer while the other kept watch.

"Okay, then," said Larry, and the session started.

"Let's begin with one of the questions on the reader's guide," said Anna. She had copied many of the questions from the Penguin edition in the back of the novel and added a few of her own. "Why does the book begin and end at the pond?"

"It's a nice place," said Donnell. "Like, a perfect place. The way the writer describes it. Lennie like to go there because it's a peaceful place. He can dream in that environment and shit."

"It's like Eden," said Larry. "In Genesis."

"It ain't all perfect like it is in the Garden of Eden," said Antonius. "Bad stuff happens there. In the end part, that little snake gets snatched out the water by that bird. Remember?"

"That's just nature," said a heavy-lidded man who spoke very softly. "The strong survive. Just like on the streets."

"The very first line of the book," said Anna, "places the setting a few miles south of Soledad. I think that the author locates it there intentionally. *Soledad* is the Spanish word for 'solitude.' Does anyone have any thoughts on what this means with regard to the novel?"

"Like, solitary?" said Antonius. "I can speak on that. I just got out."

Some of the men chuckled.

"Okay, Antonius," said Anna. "Tell us how it was. If you don't mind."

"I don't mind." Antonius, his arms folded, shrugged. "For me, solitary was fine. Peaceful. But yeah, some dudes can't deal with it. It's punishment, man. *Supposed* to be."

"In the book," said Anna, "solitude is presented as a negative thing. Many of the characters, like Candy, Crooks, and Curley's wife, talk about their profound sense of loneliness."

"Curley's wife was a straight ho," said Donnell.

"She's not getting any attention from her husband," said Anna. "She talks about her dreams of being a movie star. In fact, most of the people in the book have dreams, like George and Lennie's dream of a farm. And the dreams are unattainable."

"She still a trick," said Donnell. "I knew when she said to

Lennie 'Stroke my hair,' he was gonna break that bitch's neck. 'Scuse me, Anna."

"No, you're onto something. *How*'d you know?"

"'Cause in the very beginning of the book, Lennie killed that mouse the same way, by pettin it too hard. Same with the puppy."

"Exactly right," said Anna. "John Steinbeck was telling you ahead of time what was going to happen by using a literary device called foreshadowing."

The group grew quiet. She had gotten too professorial. The men didn't want to be schooled or talked down to. They wanted to discuss the characters and the story.

"That's the same way with Curley's dog," said Antonius, breaking the silence.

"Foreshadowing," said Michael, looking at Anna with a smile in his eyes.

"Right," said Antonius. "They took that dog out and shot him. But really, they did that dog a favor, since the rest of his life was gonna be misery. The same way George had to shoot Lennie in the end of the book."

"Lennie was a *re*-tard," said the man with the heavy-lidded eyes. "George couldn't carry him no more."

"Nah," said Antonius. "George did that thing for Lennie because Lennie was his boy. 'Cause Curley was gonna string Lennie up and lynch his ass. Or, if Lennie *did* go to prison for killin that trick, he wouldn't make it in San Quentin or wherever they'd put him out there in California, back in the old days."

"Lennie couldn't jail," said Larry.

"Exactly," said Antonius.

"You're saying," said Anna, "that George killed Lennie out of friendship."

"Yeah."

"That's what this book is about," said Michael. "Friendship and brotherhood. Companionship. The author means to say that people together are better than they are alone."

"Does anyone say that outright in the novel?" said Anna.

"Sure." Michael opened his book to where he had dog-eared a page. "I marked a spot. It's in that chapter when Crooks is talking to Lennie in Crooks's room. Can I read it?"

"Go ahead."

Michael squinted as he read. "'"A guy needs somebody—to be near him. A guy goes nuts if he ain't got nobody. Don't make no difference who the guy is, long's he's with you. I tell ya," he cried, "I tell ya a guy gets too lonely an' he gets sick."'"

"For a friend, though," said Antonius, "Lennie be buggin the *shit* out of George."

"'Tell me about the rabbits, George,'" said Donnell, in his idea of Lennie's voice.

"'Which way did they go, George, which way did they go?'" said the heavy-lidded one, and then, when no one laughed, embarrassed, he said, "Ain't none a' y'all seen that old cartoon?"

"They gonna get a farm," said Antonius, picking up on the vibe. "'An' live off the fatta the lan'!'"

Now many of the inmates laughed.

"All right." Anna picked up an article that she had printed out down in the workroom. "Let me read something to you that John Steinbeck wrote himself. It might have been from his acceptance speech when he won the Pulitzer Prize, or it might be from his journals. I don't remember which. I got it off of Wikipedia, to be honest with you. But for me it sort of speaks to this book and his worldview in general."

"Read it," said Michael, leaning forward.

"Okay," said Anna, and she began. "'In every bit of honest writing in the world there is a base theme. Try to understand men, if you understand each other you will be kind to each other. Knowing a man well never leads to hate and almost always leads to love. There are shorter means, many of them. There is writing promoting social change, writing punishing injustice, writing in celebration of heroism, but always that base theme. Try to understand each other.'"

"What if someone step to you and try to take you for bad?" said Donnell. "What you supposed to do then? Under*stand* their ass?"

"Turn the other cheek," said Larry. "It's right there in the Bible."

"An eye for an eye is in there too," said Donnell.

"The man is saying, try to do what's right," said Michael. "Reach out to other people. *Try.*"

The conversation drifted to money and fame, as it tended to do.

"Was Steinbeck rich?" said Antonius.

"I'm sure he was," said Anna. "His books were huge bestsellers. Many of them were made into movies and plays."

"I bet he got mad respect too," said Donnell.

"Not from everyone," said Anna. "Many academics don't really care for his work. They think it's too simplistic and obvious."

"You mean people could relate to it too easy."

"Well, yes. He was what's called a populist author. He wrote books that could be read and appreciated by the people he was writing *about*."

"This book was deep," said the soft-spoken man.

"Seriously, that was, like, the best chapter-book you ever gave us," said Donnell.

"Thank you, Miss Anna."

"You're very welcome," she said.

As they filed out of the chapel, Antonius tugged on Michael Hudson's jumpsuit.

"Yo, Hudson."

"What you want?"

"Got a message from our boy Phil Ornazian."

"Yeah?"

"He said to tell you everything's gonna be cool."

"That's it?"

"Short and to the point," said Antonius. "Looks like you about to go uptown."

Michael said nothing further to Antonius. He went on his way.

IN HIS cell that night, lying in the upper bunk, which he had taken for its better light, Michael Hudson read a Western novel that Anna had chosen for him. It was one of two full-length novels that were bound in the same book, part of a series called Elmore Leonard's Western Roundup. This was volume 3. He had been reading with urgency, as it was almost time for lights-out. He had just finished the novel, and its last line had given him the chills. It had jacked him up to the degree that he had gone back to the first page with the intention of reading the book again.

The name of the novel was *Valdez Is Coming*. Michael reread its first two paragraphs:

Picture the ground rising on the east side of the pasture with scrub trees thick on the slope and pines higher up. This is where everybody was. Not all in one place but scattered in small groups, about a dozen men in the scrub, the front line, the shooters who couldn't just stand around. They'd fire at the shack when they felt like it, or when Mr. Tanner passed the word, they would all fire at once.

Others were up in the pines and on the road that ran along the crest of the hill, some three hundred yards from the shack across the pasture. Those watching made bets whether the man in the shack would give himself up or get shot first.

Michael liked how the author set everything up real fast, from jump. Like, without telling you too many details, you knew right away what was happening. It gave you a feeling and made you choose a side. There is a man in a shack, and he is outnumbered and outgunned, and there are many men on the high ground, shooting down on the man who is alone, and there's a man in charge named Tanner who is giving the orders. Straight on, because most folks side with the underdog, you are hoping that someone helps the man in the shack and stops this man Tanner.

The man you think is going to help is a Mexican constable

and former soldier named Bob Valdez. He comes on the scene and does something, is tricked into it, really, that is unexpected, and then Tanner, being who he is, does the Mexican dirt. Valdez is a man who is alone, and Tanner is powerful, and he has many men backing him up. So Tanner shoves Valdez, because he can. And the more he shoves him, the harder Valdez gets, and the more he pushes back. By the end of the book, Tanner realizes that he should have given Valdez what he wanted to begin with, which was not much at all. It wouldn't have cost so much.

Picture the ground rising on the east side of the pasture…

Picture it. The author, Mr. Leonard, is *telling* you to look at it. To see it in your head. It's a bold way to start the story, but it does what it sets out to do. Michael could picture the rise of the land, and the pines, and the men in groups firing down on the one man who was cornered in his shack. And Michael could guess what wasn't on the page because of the vivid description of what was. Maybe there was a chill in the air, since they were high up in those hills. Maybe there were cotton-white clouds moving across a bright blue sky, and shadows on the pines when those clouds drifted across the sun.

Michael closed his eyes. When he read a book, he wasn't in his cage anymore. There wasn't a lock on his door, or the rank smell of the dirty commode by the bunk, or his low-ass cellmate passing gas in his sleep, or the sounds of men shouting in the unit. Guards telling him what and what not to do. He hadn't disappointed his mother. He wasn't looking at five years in a federal prison on a felony gun charge.

When he read a book, the door to his cell was open. He could step right through it. He could walk those hills under that big blue sky. Breathe the fresh air around him. See the shadows moving over the trees. When he read a book, he was not locked up. He was free.

PART II

SIX

PHIL ORNAZIAN had known Matthew Mirapaul when both of them played in bands back in the early to mid-nineties. This was around the time they were coming out of Wilson, the public high school in Ward 3, in Upper Northwest, west of Rock Creek Park. Mirapaul drummed in a hard-core band in the tradition of John Stabb's Government Issue with shades of metal à la Scream. Ornazian played bass in a band called the People's Drug that had a prominent rhythm section driving melodic, anthemic songs. At the time they were going for that Jawbox sound.

Both of their bands cut albums, not on the Dischord label. Both opened for bands like Lungfish, Circus Lupus, Nation of Ulysses, and Slant 6. Ornazian and Mirapaul played at Black Cat–level venues, and there they were not even headliners. They never made it to the stage of the 9:30 Club. But they were part of the storied D.C. scene and they had fun.

Mirapaul had aspirations. His ambition was to record for a major label, or an offshoot of one, but he never came close. He even had a stage name, Tony Leung, who was an actor in John

Woo's Hong Kong films. Mirapaul had no Asian in him, but the name change was a rock-star thing to do, and also he felt that his real name was too easily mangled.

Mirapaul was Straight Edge, Ornazian was not. When he was in bands, Ornazian was a hard drinker and ate his share of speed. But he cleaned up completely when he met Sydney, who used neither alcohol nor drugs.

In the tradition of Washington's punk-rock royalty, Mirapaul and Ornazian aged out of their bands but attempted to remain true to their ideals as adults by staying in town and working in the community. Mirapaul got his law degree, remained independent, and opened a practice as a criminal defense attorney, taking on clients who couldn't afford representation by larger firms. Ornazian got his investigator's license and found that he liked the work. Every day was different, and he wasn't caged in a room or subjected to office politics. Much of his business came from attorneys. Though he was friendly with many prosecutors, he rarely accepted work from them. Typically, he gathered evidence that defense lawyers like Mirapaul could take into court.

Somewhere along the line, Ornazian's ethics had blurred.

Mirapaul leaned back in the chair set behind his desk. He was of average height and thin. His close-cut hair had gone completely gray. His features were sharp, and his sun-creased face was as lined as a cowboy's. He wore a plain charcoal suit with an open-necked white shirt. A pre-knotted tie was looped on a nearby hanger.

"You cleaned up for me, Phil."

"When I'm calling on money," said Ornazian, seated before him.

Ornazian was wearing an American Giant blue hoodie over

a black T, and Levi's 501s cuffed up over black Wolverine boots. All of it, save the boots, was fresh out of the laundry. Mirapaul was right, Ornazian *had* cleaned up for him. He needed work.

"What do you have for me, Matt?" said Ornazian. "I hope it's something big. Could use one of those yearlong jobs you used to throw my way."

"The Tommy Winterses of this world are few and far between these days."

Tommy Winters had run a murder-for-hire outfit out of Southeast back in the early aughts. He and his lieutenants were responsible for twenty-eight murders, retribution kills, turf beefs, and the permanent silencing of witnesses who had been scheduled to testify in prominent trials. Ornazian had spent thirteen months in Congress Heights and Washington Highlands untangling the web of loyalties, betrayals, and organizational machinations. It had been Ornazian's most challenging, and lucrative, case.

The Tommy Winters job had put good money in Ornazian's pocket, but it had also permanently put him on the radar screen of major-crime-unit police and federal law enforcement officials who had been trying to nail Winters for years. Ornazian was followed, pulled over in his car for nonexistent infractions, and stared down in court. His phone was bugged by the Feds. As an investigator in the rougher sections of town, Ornazian had experienced some intimidation and near violence, but the truth of it was, he feared the DOJ and the FBI more than he feared the streets.

Mirapaul and Ornazian had worked the case hard, not because they liked Winters but because they had agreed to take his case. Despite their diligence, Winters was convicted. He had, most likely, personally committed or ordered many of the murders he had been charged with. Winters was currently doing life without parole in the supermax out in Colorado.

"So your murder business is a little off," said Ornazian. "That's kind of a good thing, right?"

"Absolutely," said Mirapaul. "The city's in pretty good shape. I live here with my family, so I couldn't be more pleased."

Ornazian swept his hand around, gesturing to the surroundings. "You're making the rent on this place, so you must be doing fine."

Mirapaul's office, located above a liquor store on C Street, near Judiciary Square and the courts, was a rather ramshackle affair, meant to impress no one. He owned a Jeep rather than a German import. The walls were not decorated with law degrees or awards but with framed photographic prints of the musicians and audiences of the original D.C. punk-rock era taken by local artists like Cynthia Connelly, Jim Saah, Lucian Perkins, and Rebecca Hammel.

"I'm not wealthy," said Mirapaul, "if that's what you mean."

"I'm not either," said Ornazian. "But I wouldn't mind trying it on for size."

"I might have something for you. Not sure if you want to take it."

"What is it?"

"You wouldn't be working for me. I know that would pain you."

"I'd get over it."

Mirapaul leaned forward and tented his hands on his desk.

"My accountant, a guy named Bill Gruen, phoned me. He has another client by the name of Leonard Weitzman, corporate attorney, lives up in Potomac. Weitzman mentioned to Gruen that he needed some investigative help."

"Concerning?"

"Weitzman's daughter, a high school sophomore at Churchill. She had a party while her parents were out of town on a getaway weekend. The party went wrong."

Ornazian opened the Moleskine notebook he'd carried in and took a pen off Mirapaul's desk. "What's the daughter's name?"

"Lisa. Apparently, the day of the party, she talked it up on Facebook and, big surprise, a lot of people showed up who hadn't been invited. Among them were a group of guys from a D.C. high school east of the river."

"No need to speak in code, Matt. You're with a friend."

"It's not what you think. It wasn't just these kids from North-east who came up to the suburbs. You had private-school boys from Potomac and Bethesda and some other guys who looked considerably older than teenage. Lisa didn't know most of these people. Neither did any of her friends, supposedly."

"Want me to guess what happened?"

"The house got tore up. I mean, whoever did it, they trashed the shit out of it. They broke a bunch of chairs and carved up a custom-made dining-room table that Weitzman says is worth tens of thousands of dollars. And they stole a whole rack of valuables from the parents' bedroom."

"Do you think drugs and alcohol were involved?"

"Gee, I don't know."

"What were they doing?"

"The usual stuff, with a twist. Weitzman said he found bottles all over the house that had the residue of purple liquid in them."

"Lean. Sizzurp. Purple Drank. Whatever the fuck they're calling it this week. These suburban kids like to emulate their favorite brain-damaged rappers."

"It gets worse," said Mirapaul. "You know what Versed is?"

"A date-rape drug."

"An amnesiac, to be precise. Someone slipped Lisa a Versed mickey."

"The daughter was raped?"

"She says she doesn't remember anything. She woke up in her bedroom with her panties on backward. Discomfort in her vaginal and anal areas. Semen residue…"

"I get it. The police did a rape kit on her, I assume."

"Weitzman didn't report it to the police."

"What the fuck?"

"He thinks it's better if the family keeps it private," said Mirapaul. "You know, the shame of it all." He let that settle in the room.

"What do you think he wants with me?" said Ornazian.

"Among the stolen items was a diamond-and-platinum Tiffany bracelet. It was a gift from Weitzman to his wife."

"Doesn't he have insurance?"

"I would think so. Give me your notebook."

Ornazian handed it to Mirapaul, who wrote something on a blank page. He pushed the notebook back across the desk.

"Give Weitzman a call," said Mirapaul. "Only if you want to. He's not a friend of mine. He's not even an acquaintance. I passed the information on to you, as I said I would. I don't care what you do but as of now, I'm out of it."

"You don't like this guy."

"I don't know him. But I have a daughter, Phil."

Ornazian stood from his chair. "What do you hear from Antonius Roberts?"

"He's in Big Sandy, the federal joint in eastern Kentucky. He got twelve. Antonius doesn't contact me, but his grandmother does. It's a fifteen-hour drive from D.C. to that prison, and she doesn't even own a car. She's not in good health, so it's a good bet that she's never gonna see him again. That's what happens to these guys in the District. There's no local prison anymore. They get shipped out all over the country. When they're gone, they're gone for real."

"What about Michael Hudson?" said Ornazian. He was careful to ask the question in an offhanded way.

"He was released. It took a while. When the witness refused to testify against Michael, the judge held him in contempt and locked him up. They were hoping to coerce his testimony but the guy wouldn't budge. I mean, he was the one who got robbed. *He* was the guy who called the police on Hudson. And suddenly he's willing to go to jail to keep his mouth shut. It's strange, Phil." Mirapaul looked Ornazian directly in the eye. "Don't you think?"

"It's a crazy, mixed-up world," said Ornazian.

Mirapaul raised an eyebrow. "Anyway. After the witness spent a few months in jail, the judge got exasperated and dismissed the case without prejudice. Meaning they could retry Hudson in the future. But he's out. The charges are still on his record but he's not carrying a felony conviction. And he didn't have to do the nickel."

"That's good. I liked that guy."

"You know, Mike took the gun charge, but he never so much as touched a gun that night. I'm happy for him. I put him in touch with a nonprofit group that counsels offenders who come out. They help them reenter society, get jobs, all that. I hope he doesn't fall back."

"So do I."

"I guess Hudson owes you a solid."

"For what?"

"The work you did on his behalf."

"I didn't do anything," said Ornazian. "The witness sprung him. It was luck."

"Don't be so modest."

"Thanks for the referral, Matt. I'll let you know if it pans out."

Ornazian left the office. Mirapaul watched him go.

SEVEN

THE DAY Michael came uptown, he moved right back into his mother's house on Sherman Avenue, between Kenyon and Lamont, in Columbia Heights. It was a typical D.C. row home, first-floor living and dining room, kitchen in the back, three small bedrooms and a bathroom upstairs. Doretha Hudson had grown up in this home. She had inherited it from her parents, who were both deceased.

Of the three Hudson siblings, Michael was the only one still in town. His older brother, Thomas, with whom he'd shared a bedroom growing up, was career military, now stationed on an army base in Texas. His kid sister, Olivia, was a senior at Virginia State in Petersburg, preparing to graduate. So he was surprised, and pleased, when his mother, Thomas, and Olivia all greeted him at the door when he arrived. Thomas had flown in to D.C. and Olivia had driven up from school.

They all hugged deeply. His longest embrace had gone to his mother and when he pulled back, tears had broken from her eyes. Inside the house, tied to a dining-room chair, there was a heart-shaped balloon she'd bought at the grocery store, and on the balloon were the words WELCOME HOME. His mother promptly served them a dinner of meat loaf, fried chicken, mashed potatoes, and greens and, for dessert, sweet potato pie. The family dog, Brandy, slept on Michael's feet while he ate.

The conversation during dinner did not go to Michael's crime or his incarceration at first. He was grateful for that. His mother, thankfully, was her typical upbeat self.

"Couple of your old runnin buddies came by while you were away," said Doretha. "They were asking on you, Michael."

"I know Mario didn't come by," said Thomas, "'cause that fool is locked up."

"I'm speaking on Chris and David," said Doretha.

"How's Junior doin?" said Michael. His old friend's name was Chris Preston Jr., but hardly anyone but his mother ever called him Chris.

"He's cooking on the Amtrak. Back and forth to and from New York, all day. Culinary school paid off."

"Cooking?" said Thomas. "You mean he's using the touch-pad on a microwave."

"It's a start," said Doretha.

"David's girl must have had their baby," said Michael.

"They had a little boy. He's living with the mother now. Says they're going to get married soon."

"He still working on his music?" said Thomas, a hint of sarcasm in his voice as he got down on a thigh.

"He's got a real job too," said Doretha. "Working at the Walmart up on Georgia Avenue."

"Hmph," said Thomas.

"I gotta get over to his place and see his kid," said Michael.

Olivia talked about the experience of leaving the city for college life "down in Virginia," and the culture change, and its challenges. She spoke on her career plans after graduation. Olivia always knew what she wanted and had plotted out a path. Michael took note of but did not speak of her weight gain while she was at school. Obviously they had fried-chicken outlets in the Commonwealth. Olivia always did love her Popeyes. Eventually, she brought up his stay in the D.C. Jail.

"Did time go slow for you in there?" said Olivia.

"I didn't mind it."

"How did you fill up your day?"

"Books," said Michael. "I got to reading and it became a habit. I read all the time."

"Weren't you scared, though?"

"No," said Michael. "I kept to myself and didn't get involved in anyone else's drama. How you *should* do."

"Both days I came to visit you, I was scared. With those doors closing behind you. The sound of it, I mean. And that lady guard who searched me before they let me in? She was rough. I mean, she put her hands in my bra and everything. She had her hands all over me."

"What you expect?" said Thomas. "Women try to bring in all kinds of contraband to their boyfriends and husbands."

"How would you know?" said Olivia. "Did you visit Michael at all when he was in the jail?"

"I didn't," said Thomas. "And you *know* I didn't. Michael's a man. I figured he'd carry it like a man. He didn't need me to come hold his hand. We got rules in society, rules you got to follow. He did a crime and he got punished for it, the way it should be." Thomas looked at his kid brother. "Am I right?"

"That must have been hard for you," said Michael. "All those words…you damn near gave a speech just now."

"Screw you, man."

"Thomas," said Doretha.

"My bad," said Thomas. "Can someone pass me those greens? They're delicious."

"I cook 'em in bacon fat," said their mother.

The siblings knew how she cooked them. She'd been doing greens the same way their whole lives.

Thomas stayed mostly silent for the rest of the meal. He had been the quiet, stoic one since childhood, and his time in the military had not changed him. Judging from his comments, he also seemed to have grown more socially conservative. This sparked no rebuttal from Michael, who was basically apolitical. Plus, it was a matter of respect to let Thomas say whatever was on his mind. Their father had been in and out of their lives, mostly out, due to issues with alcohol, so Thomas, several years Michael's senior, had played the paternal role. With his steely, insular manner, he had always seemed like a man to Michael, even when they were kids.

After dinner they went to the living room and watched a Dallas–Green Bay football contest on the cable channel that showed old games. It had been played on the frozen tundra, in the snow, and the Pack was handing Dallas its ass. They were a Redskins house, united in their hatred for the Cowboys. For Michael, it was a nice cap to an already good day.

Later, up in their old bedroom, Thomas took Michael aside for the inevitable talk. He put a large hand on Michael's shoulder and looked into his eyes.

"You straight now, right?" said Thomas. He was taller than

Michael, with very dark skin and hair shaved close to the scalp. Veins wormed across his left temple when his manner grew intense. "You through with all this nonsense?"

"I am."

"You put the old girl through some grief."

"I know it. That's what I regret more than anything. I'm not gonna go down that road again."

"Okay, then. Bring it in."

Thomas stepped forward and wrapped his strong arms around Michael. Michael felt his spine shift and heard it crack some too.

"Damn, Thomas, you about to break my back."

"You fuck up like that again," said Thomas, "I'm gonna come home and snap you in two."

Michael knew he meant it. Thomas had always had problems controlling his temper, even now, in his thirties. In fact, it had cost him his marriage. But Michael knew that Thomas's words were said in love. Michael wasn't going to mess up again. For his own self, and especially for his mother.

The next morning, Olivia drove down south, and Thomas flew back to Texas. That left Michael, his mother, and Brandy, their aging dog.

The Hudsons had adopted Brandy from the no-kill animal shelter on Oglethorpe Street and Blair Road, in Northeast. Michael, then a sophomore at Cardozo High School, had chosen Brandy, a medium-size mix of indeterminate breeds, when she limped across her cage to lick his hand. She had a cast on her rear right leg, which was healing from a fracture. Her former owner, a D.C. police officer, had broken her leg with the handle of a broom. In a separate incident, he had broken his wife's nose. In court, he beat the charges of spousal abuse but was later tried and convicted on animal abuse, which was a felony in the District. The Hudsons learned of Brandy's history only six months after she was adopted, when they read a story in the *Washington Post* about the officer's expulsion from the force. Previously, Michael had wondered why the dog ran terrified from the room whenever his mother picked up a broom.

Brandy was now thirteen and Michael was in his late twenties. The dog seemed to have grown old while he'd been away. She was stiff on her right side, as if the injury she had sustained when she was a puppy had returned. She had trouble getting up the stairs at night when it was time to follow Doretha to bed. Her tan coat had faded, she had lost weight, her muzzle was white, and she had gone deaf. But she still had the eyes of a doe.

Two days after his return, Michael filled out a form on his mother's laptop, printed it out, and left the house. Doretha was already down at the Department of Transportation, where she had worked as an administrative assistant since graduating from Strayer, the business college, thirty years ago. Michael walked up to the Petworth library on Kansas Avenue at Georgia and presented his form and his driver's license to the bearded man who sat at the desk near the front entrance. The man gave Michael a temporary library card on the spot and told him that a permanent one would be sent to him in the mail. It was his first library card.

Michael looked around him at the intricate inlaid design on the lobby floor and the hanging lights with the large glass bowls. It was a nice, freestanding brick building with a quiet, peaceful vibe. Though it was an old structure, it seemed re-done, like one of those cars that had been restored.

Michael went to the big room where they kept the fiction books. Folks of all ages sat at a long table holding keyboards and screens, doing research, or just reading random stuff on the internet. The floor in here was a nice checkerboard design, and there was an inactive fireplace at the rear of the room where people sat on comfortable furniture and read. Some of the windows gave to a view of the nicely kept football field at Roosevelt High, home of the Rough Riders. Michael spent an hour or so browsing the stacks, picking out a couple of books from the hardwood shelves. He was happy here and could have stayed all day.

At the desk, he checked out the books from the same bearded man who'd greeted him when he came in. He asked the man if they had a fiction book called *Hard Rain Falling*, by Don Carpenter. The man looked it up on a monitor and told him that they didn't have the book at that particular branch, but that they could have it transferred over to Petworth.

"I'd like that," said Michael. "Thanks."

The man scanned the bar code on the books *Lost in the City* and *The Things They Carried*, which had been one of Anna's recommendations from when Michael was locked up.

"Edward P. Jones," said the bearded man, tapping his finger on the cover of *Lost in the City*. "He went to Cardozo. Did you know that?"

"I didn't," said Michael. "I went to Cardozo too."

"There you go," said the bearded man. "Another win for the D.C. public-school system." Michael took the books off the counter and once again thanked the man for his help.

Walking back to Sherman Avenue, Michael thought of his time at Cardozo, the wasted opportunities, the teachers and administrators there who'd tried to help him along. But he was too much of a knucklehead then to listen to them or even to his mom.

There was this one teacher, O'Leary, also the school's baseball coach, who'd encouraged him to sign up for the AP English class. In that class they had this Writers in Schools program, where the students would all read a certain book, and then the author who wrote that book would come into the classroom and discuss it with the kids. That would have been cool, but Michael at that point was not a reader and lacked the confidence to give it a try. He was always good with numbers and passed his mathematics exams without even studying. But books scared him some. Books were like a foreign language he had yet to learn.

Wasn't till Anna turned him on to reading at the jail that he began to appreciate the difference books could make in someone's life. She had brought authors to the chapel, and celebrities too, the way O'Leary had brought in real writers to Michael's high school. The poet Ethelbert Miller, longtime D.C. dude, was one he remembered well. Lisa Page, an author and a creative writing professor over at GW. And that news lady on Channel 4, Wendy Rieger, a woman who didn't talk down to the inmates and looked each one of them in the eye. He knew what Miss Anna had been doing: Giving them a connection to the outside world and showing the men who were incarcerated that writers and celebrities were flesh-and-blood people. Taking the mystery out of folks like them. Saying: They're talented but they're not necessarily better than you.

They set their sights on something and they worked to get it. You can work toward something too.

Back on the concrete porch of his mother's house on Sherman, Michael sat in a rocker sofa and began to read "The Girl Who Raised Pigeons," the first short story in the book by Mr. Jones. The row house was brick, painted red, with a red-and-white metal awning over the porch and a smaller, matching metal awning above each of the three windows on the second floor. Brandy lay out on the porch by his feet. She had found a spot in the early-spring sun.

He looked out to the street. Sherman Avenue had that grassy island in the middle of it, separating the north- and south-bound lanes, which made it seem special. Across the road, on the west side of Sherman, were restored row homes topped with turrets. On the east side, the 3200 block where his mother's house sat, a large condominium building had gone up next to an old Baptist church while Michael had been in-carcerated. The upward transformation of his neighborhood was happening too quickly for his taste, but it meant that his mother's property, which she owned outright, was growing tremendously in value. His mom would retire and live comfortably for the rest of her life when she sold the house.

Presently a uniformed mailman, a lean, middle-aged man named Gerard who had been on their route for quite some time, came up the steps. When he saw Michael, a look of pleased surprise came to his face.

"How's it going, young man?"

"Sir."

"Haven't seen you for a long time."

"I been away. But I'm back now, permanent."

Gerard nodded. He knew. "Well, we need to catch up, talk about those Redskins. But not today. I got to get on it." He handed Michael some mail folded up in a magazine.

"You look good, Mr. Gerard."

"Shoot, I walk ten miles a day." Gerard turned to the side and showed Michael his flat stomach. "U.S. Postal Service *pays* me to stay in shape." It was something Gerard said often, and Michael smiled.

"Be easy, Mailman."

"Yeah, you too."

Michael watched Gerard quickstep down the block. It reminded Michael that he needed to look for work straightaway. He wasn't trying to freeload off his mother. Back in lockup, he had spoken to a lady from Open City Advocates, folks who helped juvenile offenders come back out into the world. He was a long way from being a juvenile, but this lady knew someone who knew someone, a man who ran a restaurant in Columbia Heights, who might want to talk to him about a kitchen job. But Michael didn't even have a phone, so the next thing on his list was to go out and get a new cell so people could contact him. His mother would have to help him out with that. Probably she'd need to put him on her phone contract too. She would do it. He'd let her down many times, but she'd never lost faith in him or pushed him away.

There was so much to do. He felt like he was ready.

ANNA LIVED with her husband, Rick, in a row home on the 3600 block of Warder Street in Park View, between Quebec and

Princeton, a block west of the Soldiers' Home with its wooded acreage, pond, and putting green. Theirs was a tan brick home with interesting architectural details, a porch just large enough for a single chair, and bars on the first-floor windows. A wide, clean alley paved in red brick ran behind the house.

The Byrnes were home-owning gentrifiers who had moved onto the block four years earlier and were now familiar by sight to the long-timers. Outwardly, they were accepted. Though you never knew what was in people's hearts.

Anna liked her neighborhood and most of the people they'd met there. She and Rick could walk to the bars and restaurants on Georgia, to the newish Safeway up on Randolph—an addition to the hood that had changed the game in a way that only a grocery store could—and to the refurbished library in Petworth. There was a reborn recreation center complete with a small pool, playgrounds, and a beautiful field with bleachers, steps away. Bruce-Monroe Elementary, with its crenellated, castle-like walls, was a block south. That was a plus for Rick, who was ready to have children. He felt that the school was a sign that they should stay here and try to make it work. Anna mostly let him talk about it. She wasn't sure she wanted kids yet. Or at all.

Her parents, who visited a couple of times a year, had their reservations about Anna and Rick's chosen home. They'd ask her if living here was "safe," and she reassured them that it was fine. She was no urban dilettante. When she was out at night, she was aware of her surroundings and had no liberal guilt about crossing the street to avoid groups of young men who were coming her way. Knowing where you were was simply a reality of city life. Many young couples had dogs for security, both in their homes and on their nightly walks, but Anna felt it was unfair to keep an animal alone in the house so much of the time, as she and her husband spent every weekday at work. There were street robberies, armed and strong-arm, and the occasional homicide, and every so often she would hear the pop of gunshots at night. But there were far fewer incidents of violence than there had been when they'd first moved here. In fact, there was progress citywide.

Still, she was restless. It wasn't the neighborhood; it was marriage. Rick himself was not the problem. He was smart, funny, a gentleman, and attractive in a dark Irish way. They were friends and, so far, good partners, and they were fine in bed. Rick touched all the bases, though he was somewhat of a technician and there was a sameness to his moves. She came infrequently but that's what her vibrator was for. She loved him. She got that "now it's all right" feeling when he walked into a room.

The conventions of marriage were what gave her pause. The expected milestones and progressions. Wedding ceremony, home ownership, kids, colleges, empty nest, retirement, death. The step 1, step 2, step 3 of it that, when she thought of it, bored her to tears. And then she'd laugh at herself when she questioned these things. She was married to a good man. She didn't want to be alone.

Rick came home from work after her, as he always did. He was wearing a navy-blue Brooks Brothers suit and a blue-and-red rep tie. He called it the uniform of his law firm. Rick was handsome in a grown-man way, changed from the shaggy, bearded look he'd carried off effortlessly when they first met at Emerson. When they'd go out to see bands, and she'd stand close to him in clubs, the heat radiated between them. Now he barely listened to music anymore. In his free time, he ran and played golf.

"Hey," he said. Rick embraced her and they kissed. "Good day?"

"Yes. I'm gonna take a ride, okay?"

"Sure. I'll have a run and meet you back here in, what, an hour or so?"

"Okay."

"We can grab some dinner out."

"Great."

He kissed her again. "You look good. Really good."

She was wearing shorts over spandex, a D.C. stars-and-bars T-shirt from Bureau, a skate shop on U Street, and shoes with steel shanks. "You're quick with the compliments tonight."

"That's 'cause I want something."

"Hmm."

She climbed onto her Cannondale road bike and pedaled down the steep hill of Georgia, past the Banneker public pool where she swam during lap time in the summer months. She was hurtling straight down the edge of the Piedmont Plateau, and it would be a bitch to return on, but it was a good hard way to end a ride. She'd go downtown to the Mall and if she was ambitious, she'd do the loop at Hains Point, then come back home. They'd shower and maybe walk over to Eleventh Street to one of those restaurant/bars, then come back to the house and watch some Netflix, and at the end of the night they'd make love, that "something" he'd mentioned. It would be a good night. And, also, routine.

Pedaling hard, she thought of work, as she tended to do

while on her rides. The Mental Health unit was on the schedule for the next day, and its inmates had different needs and presented different challenges than those on the other blocks. She had staged them earlier in the afternoon and would make some additions the next morning. And then she thought about Gen Pop, which would meet the following day, and what those men would need. That guy Donnell, crafty and smart, and the born-again Christian who looked at her in ways she could not decipher, and Michael Hudson...but oh, yeah, Michael, one of her favorite clients, was no longer in the unit. One day he simply wasn't there. She didn't know if he had transitioned to a federal facility or if he'd been released.

This was something she had gotten used to. The jail held pretrial felons, pretrial misdemeanants, and sentenced misdemeanants. It wasn't a prison. No one stayed too long. She got comfortable with being around many of these men, and in some cases she looked forward to seeing them. And then they were gone.

She wondered about Michael. She hoped he'd landed well.

EIGHT

THE WEITZMAN residence was in Potomac, Maryland, off of Falls Road, in a neighborhood of split-level and Colonial homes built in the 1970s. By modern standards, the lots and structures were modest, none approaching the large acreage and square footage of houses in places like Howard County and in communities like McLean, across the river. But the big-ticket imports in the driveways and the highly rated public schools in the zip code told a story of quiet wealth.

Phil Ornazian was seated in a small room off the kitchen, his notebook, pen, and a glass of water before him, talking to Leonard Weitzman, sitting across the table from him. Weitzman's wife, Diane, sat on a stool in the kitchen at a kind of breakfast bar, having a glass of chardonnay. She was within earshot of the conversation but had elected to situate herself away from the men.

"Where'd you two go that weekend?" said Ornazian.

"The Hyatt down in Cambridge," said Weitzman. "On the Eastern Shore. Just Diane and me. We like to get away when we can."

"Do you play golf?" The resort featured an eighteen-hole course overlooking the Choptank River.

"I don't go down there for that," said Weitzman. "We go because Diane likes the atmosphere."

"They have wonderful spa facilities," said Diane.

"But you play," said Ornazian to Weitzman.

"Sure," said Weitzman, and then, offhandedly, "I'm at Congressional."

The initiation fee at Congressional Country Club was in the neighborhood of two hundred and fifty thousand dollars. It told Ornazian, and the world, that Weitzman had fuck-you money. Also, Weitzman, a Jew, had elected to join Congressional over Woodmont, the traditional Jewish club on Rockville Pike, whose initiation fee, eighty K, was considerably less. Ornazian didn't know what any of this meant, but, as he had always been outside the tent of money and power, he found it interesting.

"In retrospect," said Weitzman, "I wish we hadn't left Lisa here alone that weekend. We've done it before, but that was when her older brother lived here."

"Richard's away at Penn State," said Diane.

"She never gave us any reason to distrust her," said Weitzman, who put up his hands as if in surrender. "She never did anything like this."

That you know of, thought Ornazian. He had read up on Weitzman, who was a highly compensated chief counsel complete with stock options for a large tech company on the I-270 corridor. Weitzman might have been in denial about his daughter, or perhaps he was simply being defensive about his absence on the weekend in question, but he was a man in his fifties who had raised two teenagers, and he couldn't have been naive.

Leonard Weitzman was an average-size man with the normal weight issues of the middle-aged. He probably went to the gym regularly, but he was losing the fight. His scalp was visible through his thinning hair. At seven in the evening, he was still wearing work clothes, and they were expensive. An Armani tie, Gucci horse-bit loafers, a fine-fabric suit. Ornazian guessed he favored the Saks men's store over Nordstrom and that a clothier with a Brit accent picked out Weitzman's threads in advance of his visit. Ornazian was projecting, but some version of that scenario had to be true.

His wife, Diane, short and sturdy, was put together nicely. Her clothing was up to the minute and her hair was stylishly cut. She had all the looks and upkeep that money could buy, but tonight the blur of alcohol and undisguised stress was in her eyes.

"Tell me how the party got noticed," said Ornazian.

"Lisa announced it on Facebook," said Weitzman. "It could have spread there or it could have been a situation where, you know, people hear about it and start calling their friends. In my day, a party got around by word of mouth."

"Is Lisa still on social media?"

"She's using her laptop. She's smart enough to know not to do anything like that ever again."

"And she still has her phone."

"I'm not going to take her phone away from her. We wouldn't be able to reach her."

Ornazian picked up his pen. "I'm going to need the names of some of Lisa's close friends. People who were at the party who you know wouldn't have participated in the destruction or the theft."

Weitzman made eye contact with his wife and then looked back at Ornazian. "That's going to be tricky," he said.

"Why?"

"I described the events of that night in detail to the attorney you work for. I assume Mr. Mirapaul relayed all of it to you."

"He told me what he knew."

"Then you know that Lisa was assaulted that night. You must also know how delicate the situation is. Do you have children, Mr. Ornazian?"

"I do. The complexity of this isn't lost on me. But I'm also wondering why you didn't call the police."

"Lisa insisted we keep this quiet. She didn't want this to blow up any more than it already has. She's only a sophomore. She has to deal with the kids in her high school for two and a half more years."

"So you didn't notify the police about the robbery either."

"No."

"Weren't you concerned about Lisa's health?"

"We took her to our family gynecologist. There was some bruising but no permanent damage."

"You mean no *physical* damage."

"That's right." A touch of indignation had flared up in Weitzman's voice. "Can we move on?"

Ornazian nodded. He was pushing Weitzman's buttons for no good reason, and he told himself to stop. He suspected that Weitzman's desire to sweep his daughter's assault under the rug was as much about his own reputation as it was about hers.

With regard to the matter at hand, that was neither here nor there. Ornazian needed the job.

"Do you have a list of the stolen items?" said Ornazian.

Weitzman pushed a manila folder across the table. Ornazian opened the file. The top sheet was a printed list itemizing the goods taken from the house the night of the party, along with their estimated worth. Naturally, Ornazian wondered if the figures were inflated.

"Are these goods insured?" said Ornazian, keeping his eyes on the paper.

"Why are you asking?"

"Insurance companies send out investigators in cases involving high-dollar losses. I'd like to know if someone else is out there trying to do the same thing I am."

"That's not pertinent," said Weitzman. The lawyer in him was coming out.

Again, Ornazian made no rebuttal. He studied the list. The big ticket was the Tiffany bracelet. Its value was declared at fifty thousand dollars.

"Do you have photographs of the items?" said Ornazian.

"They're also in the folder."

Ornazian slid the list back into the folder and put it beside his notebook. "So you have no idea who did this. And none of the kids who were here have come forward?"

"We haven't asked them," said Weitzman. "That would involve the parents and, frankly, it's a bridge I didn't want to cross. There's something else too."

"Go ahead."

"Whoever did this to my house, to my daughter…these were very violent people. They cracked the granite countertop in the kitchen. They carved up my dining-room table with what had to be a very formidable knife. I don't want any of this coming back on my family."

"Understood."

"I told Mr. Mirapaul about the purple drink that was all over the house, in those bottles…"

"Promethazine and codeine. It's typically mixed with Sprite or Mountain Dew. Cranked-up cough syrup, basically. Gets you all kinds of twisted. Lisa might have had some, but it's not what knocked her out."

"I know. The doctors detected benzos in her blood."

Diane sighed audibly, shook her head, and went to the Sub-Zero for a refill on her chardonnay. She told them she was going upstairs, and they waited for her to do so.

"Mr. Mirapaul said you could help me," said Weitzman after his wife had left the room.

"I work my cases hard if I take them," said Ornazian.

"What's your fee?"

"I'll require a one-thousand-dollar nonrefundable retainer. Cash. On a job like this one, I take fifty percent of the value of any items recovered. If nothing is recovered, I get nothing."

"Why cash?"

"I might have to break some eggs. This way, the trail won't lead back to you."

"Your recovery percentage is steep."

"It is."

"The Tiffany bracelet was a twenty-fifth-anniversary present to Diane. It has a great deal of meaning for both of us."

"I'll do my best to get it back. Do we have an agreement?"

"Yes."

Ornazian picked up his notebook and the folder and got up out of his seat. "Do you mind if I look around?"

"There's not much to see. We cleaned up the house pretty well. The chairs they broke have gone out for repair. But let me show you something."

Ornazian followed Weitzman into the open kitchen. Weitzman pointed to an island with a cracked granite top. "I don't even know how you could do this." He made a head motion. "Come with me."

They walked into a dining room with walls painted a deep red. A table dominated the room. Several chairs were missing from the set. Weitzman pulled back the tablecloth to reveal a rich mahogany top badly damaged by deep carvings made with a heavy knife blade. Aside from random plow lines and the usual, unimaginative *Fuck You,* the number 14 was carved into the table. Ornazian was familiar with the number's significance but made no comment. He used his phone to take photographs of the table.

"May I speak with Lisa now?" said Ornazian.

"She said she'd talk to you. I'm going to ask that you not discuss the assault with her."

"Agreed," said Ornazian.

Weitzman produced his cell and speed-dialed his daughter.

NINE

LISA WEITZMAN, a thin girl with shoulder-length, expertly dyed blond hair, sat in a big cushioned chair on the family's back deck, which was tricked out with an array of comfortable outdoor furniture and the requisite freestanding fire pit. Ornazian sat on a bench beside her, taking notes.

Lisa wore jeans and a Canada Goose coat over a loose-fitting shirt. It was almost sixty degrees out and the down coat was not necessary today or often in Washington's mostly moderate climate, but it was the current must-own label for status-conscious people, whether they needed the warmth it provided or not. Ornazian had once been in Bloomingdale's in Chevy Chase and seen multiple customers wearing the jackets on a warm late-winter day.

Lisa was smoking an American Spirit blue-label in full view of her father, who was still in the kitchen, pretending that he was not watching them. Smoking was probably now low on the list of parental concerns with regard to his daughter.

"Tell me about the crowd that night," said Ornazian. "Who you knew, who you didn't know."

"It was a bunch of people from Churchill, originally," said Lisa, naming her public high school. "Not all of them were my best friends, but they were people I knew."

"Some close friends there too?"

"A couple."

"Do you think I could speak to them?"

"I don't know."

"Are they girls?"

"Yeah."

"Okay. What about the people you didn't know? Can you describe them or name any of them?"

"No, I can't *name* them. I'm not holding anything back. I just don't know their names."

"Describe them."

Lisa dragged on her cigarette and casually ashed her jeans. "These two guys came up from D.C. They told some of my friends that they went to Woodson, wherever that is."

"It's a public high school in Northeast. Did they cause the trouble?"

"They seemed all right. I don't know. They found out about the party on Facebook, and I think they just came to try to talk to some white girls. The guys from my school were more intimidated by them than the girls were."

"You say you don't know if they were all right."

"The night for me was split into two parts," said Lisa. "The part I remember and the part that's totally blacked out. It was like, I don't know…"

"You were drugged."

"The doctor said I was. So I didn't see any of the bad stuff that happened. I didn't see the house getting trashed or anyone stealing anything. That was toward the end of the night. I was out of it by then."

"Let's go back to what you remember. Tell me more about the kids you didn't know."

"Well, there were some guys from the private schools. They go to, like, Landon and Bullis. I've seen them around at Montgomery Mall and other parties. Most of them don't live in this neighborhood. They're from, like, Bethesda and maybe from the good parts of D.C."

"You don't know their names either."

"No."

Ornazian couldn't ascertain if Lisa was lying. Pressing her would probably shut her down. He was getting information that was helpful, so he kept the interview on the nonconfrontational track.

He said, "Who else?"

"There were these older guys who showed up."

"How much older?"

"In their twenties?"

"Did you know them?"

"Never seen them before that night," said Lisa. "They came in with the purple drink."

"Describe them."

"I don't know. White guys, and all of them were kinda tall. They were pretty jacked. They had ink and one of them had that haircut. You know, the way the guys wear their hair in, like, Brooklyn and stuff? Kinda shaved on the sides and long on top?"

"These older dudes brought the Lean?"

"Yeah, they were carrying it in a cardboard case, like a case of beer. The bottles had labels on them, the kind you'd get at a pharmacy. They were selling it to the kids."

"So people were getting messed up on the drink. What else were they doing?"

"Like, drugs?"

"Yeah."

"The usual. Smoking weed, drinking. Doing molly…"

"Licking it off their fingers?"

She shook her head. "Molly water. We mix a little in water now and drink it."

"Were you doing molly that night?"

"No, I don't like it. I smoked some tree and drank some Lean, and that's it. I'm saying, I sipped some Drank and that's the last thing I remember."

"Drank?"

"It's what we call it."

"I'm kidding you."

"Anyway. When I woke up, it was like four in the morning. Everyone was pretty much gone."

Ornazian had been writing but now he rested his pen. Lisa was smoking down her cigarette and looking away. Outwardly, she didn't seem too damaged. She was putting on a game face. But he had her attention, and despite his promise to Weitzman, he had to ask.

"Lisa, do you know who assaulted you?"

"No."

"Was it the older guys who crashed the party?"

"I don't *know*."

"Your friends must know. Some of your friends must know who trashed your parents' house and stole their valuables."

"They won't talk to you. They don't want to get involved. They don't want their parents to know what they were doing."

"Don't they want to help us find the guys who did this to you?"

"Look, I'm sorry for what happened to the house," said Lisa. "I'm sorry we got robbed. I really feel bad about what it did to my parents, and I told them so. But I'm fine. Really. I'm *fine*."

"Okay. Do me one favor. Friend me on Facebook. Help me out here. Give me a chance to retrieve your mom's jewelry."

Lisa lit a fresh cigarette off the one that was burning down and then crushed the butt under her shoe. "Gimme your phone."

Ornazian opened the Facebook app on his iPhone, went to his home page, and handed the phone over to Lisa.

"Put your contact information in there too," said Ornazian.

She produced her own cell and deftly executed the friend exchange, squinting against the smoke that was rising up off the cigarette dangling from her mouth. She then entered her contact info into Ornazian's phone and handed it back to him.

"I appreciate you talking to me," said Ornazian. "I know it must be rough."

Lisa held out her pack of American Spirits to Ornazian. Ornazian waved the offer away.

"You don't want one?"

"I gave it up a long time ago."

"These aren't as bad for you as regular cigarettes."

"They're *all* bad for you."

He stood up and shook her hand firmly. She seemed surprised by the adult gesture, and somewhat pleased.

"Thank you," said Ornazian. "If you remember anything else or if one of your friends wants to come forward…or if, you know, you just want to talk…give me a call."

"Please don't bother my friends," said Lisa.

"Don't worry," he said, and he walked back toward the house.

BY THE front door, Leonard Weitzman handed Ornazian an envelope containing one thousand dollars in cash. Ornazian slipped it into the manila folder containing the list of stolen items and the photographs.

"How did you find Lisa?" said Weitzman.

"She seems pretty strong."

"I don't think anything like this will happen again. She made a big mistake putting this on Facebook. She knows it."

Ornazian knew that Facebook had become the social media platform for middle-aged users, the elderly, and others who were settled in life. Teenagers generally used more secure and secretive platforms to communicate. By using Facebook to announce the party, Lisa had wanted the news to get out to lurkers and strangers. She was being adventurous, but not devious. She couldn't have anticipated what would happen that night.

"Do you need anything else from me?" said Weitzman.

"I've got enough to start."

"Ornazian…what is that, Middle Eastern?"

"*Near* East. I'm of Armenian descent. My great-grandparents fled the genocide. The one the Turks claim didn't happen."

"We have something in common," said Weitzman. "My

mother is a Holocaust survivor. She was a teenager in the camps. My father was army infantry. At the end of the war, he liberated her. I was the youngest of their four children. My mother is still alive. Now she has eight grandchildren and several great-grandchildren. It's quite a story, isn't it?"

"It's the American story."

"I have your contact information," said Weitzman.

"And I have yours," said Ornazian. "I'll stay in touch."

"Please respect our wishes," said Weitzman. "Keep this as quiet as possible. Don't involve the other kids or their parents."

"I won't," said Ornazian. But he already had a plan, and his assurance was a lie.

TEN

A WEEK after he'd come home, Michael Hudson decided it was time to see about a job. The lady from Open City Advocates had given him the name of a man who was the general manager of a restaurant in Columbia Heights. She'd told Michael, confidentially, that this man had a conviction from when he was younger, a possession/distribution thing that had bought him jail time in Maryland, and that he would probably be empathetic toward someone who was trying to get it together on the outside.

Michael let Brandy out into the small dirt-and-weed yard at the back of their home and waited for the dog to do her business. The yard led to an alley and an empty lot, where another east–west alley came to a T. There Michael saw four men smoking weed, talking, not bothering anyone, not doing much at all. One of them, an army veteran named Woods, was seated on a crate. Michael nodded to Woods, whom he knew from childhood, and Woods said, "Hudson," and another man said, "All right."

Brandy took her sweet time sniffing and pooping, and

Michael didn't rush her. Eventually, he had to go down into the yard, pick the dog up in his arms, and carry her back up the concrete steps into the house. Brandy got anxiety, paced in a circle, when she felt she couldn't make it up those steps. Once inside, she tottered over to her bed, a large cushion set next to Doretha's favorite armchair, and settled into a nap.

Michael dressed in a collared shirt, freshly laundered jeans, and a pair of low black Air Force Ones that he had polished. He grabbed his NYRB paperback edition of *Hard Rain Falling* and left the house. His plan was to talk to the restaurant man and then maybe find a bench in the sun and read some. The blossoms had come early after a warm winter and it would be nice to sit outside. He was deep into his book.

He walked over to Eleventh Street around Park Road, where there was a cluster of restaurants, bars, and coffee shops on the otherwise residential block. He passed Tubman Elementary, where kids were kicking a ball around on the field. Nearby was a fenced-in area where dogs played and their owners socialized.

The restaurant was on a corner of the intersection and took up the entirety of a three-story row house that was topped with a turret, D.C.'s signature architectural feature. There was outdoor seating, picnic tables mostly, up on a patio, where Christmas lights had been strung. Alongside the patio was a small porch with a metal cage holding stacks of split wood, and steps led down to double doors, which Michael guessed was access for food deliveries. The sign outside the place said THE DISTRICT LINE. And below it, in smaller letters, GOOD FOOD AND DRINK.

Michael went inside.

A young woman with ginger-colored hair was behind the bar, slicing fruit. The bar ran from the entrance to the rear of the room, where a hall led to a stairwell. A man in street clothes, wearing a short brown apron tied around his waist, was setting silverware on bare wooden tables. There weren't many tables, and the place was empty of customers.

"Hi," said the bartender to Michael. She had a nice smile.

"Hello."

"We're not serving yet. Lunch starts in about a half hour."

"I'm here to see…" Michael looked down at the notepaper he was using as a bookmark in the novel he was carrying. Its top peeked out of the pages. "Angelos. We got an appointment."

"He's down in the kitchen. He'll be right up."

Almost as she said it, a barrel-chested man in his early thirties came out of the stairwell and appeared in the room, carrying magnum bottles of white wine in a box. He set the box on the bar. He had a heavy black beard and wore a red bandanna over his longish black hair. He looked like a well-fed pirate.

"This man is here to see you, Angelos."

"Michael Hudson." Michael stepped forward and put out his hand. Angelos shook it.

"Angelos Valis." He looked at his wristwatch, a rotary-faced job with a green band, and said, "Let's go upstairs. It's quiet there." To the bartender he said, "Call me if you need me, Callie."

Michael followed Angelos up a narrow set of stairs by the front door to another dining room that was also on the small side, a corner room with windows all the way around, looking down on Eleventh. They had a seat at a two-top. Michael put his book down on the table. Again Angelos looked at his watch.

"Thanks for seeing me," said Michael.

"You come recommended by the woman over at Open City. They're good people, so that goes in your favor. But I need to know a few things before this conversation goes any further. Specifically, your priors. Not just convictions. Charges too."

"You get right to it."

"We're about to open. So tell me. You just got out."

"I was charged with armed robbery, but the charges got dropped. The man who was robbed decided not to testify."

"You had a gun?"

"No, my partner did. I was there to back him up and drive the car. When a heater's involved, doesn't matter who's carrying it. You still take the gun charge."

"I guess you've been told that I'm no stranger to lockup. So it doesn't bother me that you've been in jail. But I won't hire a violent offender or a sex offender. I just won't."

"I've never done anything like that."

"My friend said you had other priors."

Michael hesitated. Angelos had looked him in the eye the entire time he'd been with him. He was direct, but that was cool. Michael wasn't offended. This dude was straight.

"Well?"

"I was into cars when I was young. I stole one once and got probation. When I stole another one, I got sent to juvenile."

"New Beginnings?"

"Nah, that wasn't open yet. I was out there in Oak Hill."

"That's rough."

"*Yeah*, it was."

"How old are you?"

"I'm twenty-eight."

"That's a long gap between your juvenile priors and the commission of a robbery ten years later. Why'd you decide to commit another crime?"

"I was stupid," said Michael. "But I'm not gonna be stupid anymore."

Angelos continued to look into Michael's eyes and Michael did not cut his eyes away.

"You ever work in a restaurant before?" said Angelos.

"No," said Michael. "But I'll learn."

"What are you good at?"

"Numbers. I used to work store jobs. Like, in D.C.? The sales tax is five and three-quarters percent. You can give me any amount, and I can do that tax in my head. Don't need to look it up."

"That's great, but I don't need someone to operate the register or wait tables. Do you speak Spanish?"

"No," said Michael.

"Well, that's a problem right there. You'd be working in the kitchen. My kitchen crews are Hispanic and for the most part they don't speak English. Anyone who works down there has to be able to communicate with them."

"You sayin you don't hire no one but Spanish?"

"That's pretty much the case. Look, they seem to be the only ones who want these jobs, and they work the hell out of them. If one of them can't come in, they send in a friend or a relative to cover. I'm never shorthanded."

"You're telling me that you have an opening in the kitchen?"

"Dishwasher," said Angelos. "Actually, it's not open yet. One of the guys I have now has a problem with alcohol. I can't carry him anymore. I'm going to let him go on payday."

"Look, I need a job," said Michael. "Saying, I want *this* job. I can do it. You can count on me, for real. I'll learn to talk with those people somehow. Can't be that difficult, right?"

"Let me think about it," said Angelos.

"You don't need to think on it," said Michael. "You already know. I don't want to leave outta here without an answer. Can I have this job? Why don't you just tell me? Yes or no?"

Angelos chuckled. "You're aggressive."

"Well?"

Angelos thought it over, then nodded. "On the day shift you'd work mostly with the ladies. They have to get their kids late in the afternoon. The hombres work at night. Except for Joe, little macho guy, likes to box. He's on days too. We have a wood-fired oven. One of your duties would be splitting the wood that gets fed into the oven."

"I can do that. I saw the logs outside."

"Pay-wise, you'd start at the bottom. Minimum wage is eleven fifty an hour in the District. It goes up to twelve fifty in July. It'll be thirteen fifty a year after that."

"That works."

"Write down your cell number for me."

"I'm fixin to get one. I'll give you the landline number at my mother's house."

Michael pulled out his makeshift bookmark, dog-eared the page where it had been, and used Angelos's pen to write down his mother's home number. He pushed the piece of paper across the table.

"Good book," said Angelos, nodding at the cover of *Hard Rain Falling*. "Like, *seriously* good. I read it when I was locked up in Clarksburg. That's all I did out there was read.

Still remember the librarian's name. We called her Miss Margaret."

"I'm halfway into it," said Michael. "Curious to see how it's gonna end up."

"Not how you'd expect," said Angelos.

"Thank you," said Michael. "I won't let you down."

They shook hands.

"Get a cell phone," said Angelos.

Michael nodded. "I'm *about* to."

MICHAEL WENT back down to the bar and took a seat. Angelos had told Callie to take care of him, so he ordered a Margherita pizza and a glass of ice water and observed the operation as the modest lunch crowd streamed in. Callie and the one waiter handled the whole service. A runner, one of the kitchen ladies, delivered the food to the dining room from the basement, and a short man with slicked-down hair, who Michael assumed was the dishwasher, brought up glassware to the bar and went back down to the hole with bus trays. Callie, the bartender, controlled the music, which today alternated between reggae and something like country. A flat-screen TV hung over the bar showed a soccer game with the sound turned off. The atmosphere was chill. Seemed to Michael that they had it all wired up tight. While he ate, his neighborhood mailman, Gerard, came in with the daily delivery. He and Michael exchanged some friendly words.

The pizza tasted fresh. He left Callie a few dollars and told her he'd see her soon.

Michael walked over to Georgia and Upshur Street. There was a brand-new diner there that had opened since he'd been away, and different kinds of folks were sitting in booths and at the counter, having lunch. All kinds of new places here, table-cloth restaurants and bars mixed with the old barbershop and two funeral homes, the longtime Strange Investigations office, and a couple of neighborhood markets.

He walked farther and went into a small bookstore on Upshur that he had noticed but not yet visited. He looked around at the selection and then went to the register and talked to an attractive young woman with a diamond stud in her nose who had a welcoming smile.

"I was wondering if you could help me," said Michael. "I used to have this book in a series called Elmore Leonard's Western Roundup. Volume number three. It was two books in one. Can I order that from you?"

The young woman looked it up on her computer. "That series is out of print. But the novels in that particular volume are available separately in paperback. *Valdez Is Coming* and *Hombre*. Right? I can get those for you if you'd like."

"How much would that be?"

She looked at the screen and told him the price. Michael had some walking-around money in his pocket that his mother had given him, and this was an extravagance, but he wanted to celebrate.

"Go ahead and order them," said Michael. "I could get those books at the library across the street, but I'd rather have them permanent. I'm gonna start my *own* library."

"That's great."

"I got a job today," he said, as if she'd asked.

"Congratulations."

Michael gave her his name and his mother's landline number so that she could contact him when the books came in.

"What's your name?" he said.

"Anna."

"I got a friend name Anna who likes books too."

"Nice to know I'm not the only one." The young woman smiled. "I'll call you when these come in, Michael."

"See you soon. This here is gonna be my spot."

He found a bench nearby and read for a while, then walked back toward his mother's house on Sherman. A couple blocks north of his home, he saw a woman he knew from high school getting out of her road-worn Hyundai. Michael remembered her as Carla. She was with a little girl, preschool age, had tiny seashells in her braids. Carla held her little girl's hand and smiled as Michael approached them.

"Hey."

"Carla Thomas," said Michael. "Like the singer."

"It's me."

Michael looked down at the child and spoke softly. "How you doin, baby girl? You look pretty today."

"Thank you," she said, and she leaned her face shyly against her mother's leg.

Carla was tall with pretty brown eyes, large-boned, but he liked that. She was put together on a low budget. Wasn't wearing designer stuff, but her hair and makeup were nice and she smelled good. Carla cared enough about herself to keep it tight. Michael had liked her back at Cardozo, thought she was attractive and funny, but for whatever reason they had never hooked up.

"Where you been?" said Michael. "I ain't seen you in years. Heard you moved out to *Mer*'land."

"I was in P.G. for a minute, but I didn't like it. That wasn't a place for Alisha," she said, nodding at her daughter. "It's safer here in the city. I moved back in with my grandmother, for now. Alisha's about to go to Tubman next year, so we'll see."

"Hmm."

"What *you* doin, big man?"

"Working," he said. "I'm at that restaurant, the District Line, up on Eleventh?"

Her eyes registered relief, and interest, when he told her he had a steady job.

"That's good."

"My name's Michael, by the way," he said.

"I know your *name.*"

"You didn't call me by it."

"You didn't give me a chance."

"We should get together sometime," said Michael, boldly.

"Hard for me to get out. What with the classes I'm taking, and my job, and my little girl…"

"Okay, then. I understand."

"I didn't say I couldn't. Just said it was hard."

Michael looked her over. "You look good, girl."

"So do you."

"I'm maintaining."

"So what now?"

"I'll come past."

They exchanged a smile, and Michael went on his way.

* * *

LATER, SITTING on his porch and reading his book, Brandy sleeping at his feet, Michael felt flush with anticipation. The new job was a start. This time his life would be different, because he would make it so. He needed to remember, going to work every day, keeping your head down, that was how most folks made it. Inch by inch. He didn't need to be looking at things he couldn't afford. Wasn't any right way to get those things fast. He had to be like one of those racehorses with blinders on. Keep looking straight ahead, no distractions. Keep focused on the task at hand.

Now he had to go over to the electronics store on Fourteenth with his mom and get a new cell. The store had a deal right now for a free smartphone if you signed up for the service. His mother was cool. She would put him on her plan.

ELEVEN

PHIL ORNAZIAN sat on the second-floor sleeper porch of his house, alternately working and looking out over the yards backing to the red-brick alley running behind Taylor. He had brought an old Ikea desk and chair out onto the porch, which served as his office for half the year, though mostly he worked out of his car. The walls of the porch had removable glass panels that he replaced with screens in the spring. Sometimes, on summer nights, he and Sydney slept out here on a futon he'd purchased in his bachelor days. Sometimes he'd let the boys join them in their sleeping bags. The porch had closed the deal for him when he'd first looked at the house.

He had been on his laptop for most of the morning, studying Facebook pages and then using his own people-finder program to locate the participants of the Weitzman party. Lisa had announced the party as a private event rather than a public event. That meant it didn't go out to the world at large but still reached her friends who could telephone it to acquaintances and strangers. There had been much chatter on her page in anticipation of the party, with many replies. Lisa had opened the doors unwittingly to bad people, but her move had also given Ornazian plenty of information to seek out the offenders. He'd made a couple of phone calls and he'd spent some time on the DC.gov website and did a search on its real property tax database. He used school-group pages and the process of elimination when common names occurred, and after several hours on his laptop he had compiled a working list of contacts, focusing on those he thought he could squeeze. He had what he needed now to start.

Ornazian sat back in his chair. The roof of the small garage at the edge of his yard, which he used as a workshop, was covered in autumn's fallen leaves. He'd need to get out back and clear it. Also trim the rosebushes and turn the soil in Sydney's vegetable garden in prep for her annual planting. Shovel up the minefield of dog poop that had accumulated in the yard. But first he had to fill the house checkbook. That was priority one.

One of his dogs barked loudly, and Ornazian said, "Hey." Blue and Whitey, lazily named for the color of their coats, sat by the rear screens looking out at the yard. They were pit-bull mixes adopted from the Humane Rescue Alliance across from the big community garden off Blair Road. Sixty- or seventy-pound bitches, still in their relative youth, mostly muscle. They'd been with him all morning. They liked to come out here and study the many dogs in the neighboring yards down in the alley. Ornazian wondered if they dreamed of playing with them or of tearing them apart.

Sydney appeared in the doorway. She was wearing black tights under a denim shirt. Her hair was in short twists. She was unkempt and she looked lovely.

"Can the boys come out, love?" she said. "They've been dying to."

"Sure. I'm done for now."

Presently his sons, Gregg and Vic, rushed out onto the porch. Both of them had gotten their feet into Ornazian's shoes and were wearing them clumsily. Their hair was curly and their skin tone was a shade lighter than their mother's. They both had Sydney's big brown eyes.

"Careful," said Ornazian as Gregg, the elder at four and a half, tripped and held on to his father's arm. Vic, the more coordinated of the two, younger than Gregg by fourteen months, had swaggered into the room more smoothly.

The dogs got up and walked around the boys in a circling-the-wagons move. Then Whitey, as she tended to do, sat down with her body leaned against Sydney's leg, always her protector.

"Bang-bang," said Vic, pistoling his hand and pointing it at his father.

"Victor," said Sydney. "You know what we say about guns."

"Yeah, Vic," said Ornazian, without conviction. He had a trigger-locked .38 in the nightstand by his bed, registered and legal due to his CCW, the license to carry in the District. He also owned a pump-action Remington, not legal, which he kept unloaded and leaning against the wall of his closet behind his hanging shirts. He hoped to never use either of them. But if anyone entered his home and came up to the second floor, where his family slept, he would.

The entrance of the kids and the excitement of the dogs told Ornazian that he wouldn't be getting any meaningful work done. His cell phone, set behind his laptop, lit up with a message. Sydney read the message over his shoulder without guilt.

It was from a woman named Monique. The message was wordless and consisted only of two symbols: a dollar sign and a question mark.

"One of your whores?" said Sydney.

"She'd probably prefer that you call her an escort."

"What's a whore, Dad?" said Gregg.

"A lady who works very hard."

"Like Mum?"

Ornazian pocketed his cell and stood up. "I've got to go."

"Aren't you going to answer your son?" said Sydney.

He kissed her mouth. "Gonna be out for the rest of the day. I'll stay in touch."

ON MONIQUE'S old Backpage listing, recently taken down, her photos showed her mostly from the rear, bending over a bed, displaying her ample behind in a thong, or in obstructed profile, pinching the elongated nipples of her breasts. Listed along with her measurements was a menu of her services, vaguely but cleverly described; the ad noted that she was available for out-call dates and that she accepted tips. She had a nice face, if one was not turned off by large features, so she was not hiding her grille out of shame or for deception but rather to conceal her identity. In addition to working as a prostitute, Monique had a straight job. She was one of the nice-looking, put-together women who worked the makeup counters at the high-end department stores clustered on Wisconsin Avenue in Friendship Heights. There were others like her in those same kinds of positions, living two lives.

Ornazian and Monique were seated at the bar of Matisse, a French restaurant on Wisconsin and Fessenden that was a quiet, refined spot for locals. Monique was having a glass of dry white wine. Ornazian stuck with water. He had passed her an envelope containing one thousand dollars in cash soon after they arrived.

"You made me ask for it," said Monique.

"I wasn't holding out on you. I've been busy."

"How'd Theodore take it?"

"Like a man. But he talked too much."

"Sounds like him. His silver tongue is forked, but that's how he gets his women."

"You know Theodore means 'God's gift,'" said Ornazian. "It's from the Greek."

"Hmph," said Monique.

Monique was wearing all black, the uniform for her day job, and she was perfectly made up, befitting her job as a specialist. She was on her lunch break and not far from the store. Ornazian asked her how it was going for her since the government had pressured Backpage to remove its escort listings.

"I'm up on another site," said Monique. "Ain't no thing to me. Always gonna be a market for what I do and a way for men to find me."

"You still working the clubs?"

"VIP rooms only," she said. "Everything's cool."

She had started as a dancer in the topless club on New York Avenue, near the dog shelter, which had once been the most bumping spot of its kind in D.C. She was out-call exclusively now, and she had no pimp. In her world, she had moved way up.

"I might have something for you," said Monique. "Could be good."

"Talk about it."

"Girl I work with up at the makeup counter? Beautiful girl, goes by Lourdes? Used to work the houses but got herself out. She got a friend named Marisol who's in a brothel in Columbia Heights, near a bar owned by this dude Gustav."

"You saying Gustav owns the brothel too."

"Right."

"What's the story with Marisol?"

"She was trafficked. Got sold to a recruiter in Guatemala and then smuggled into America, same trail they use for guns and drugs. She working off her debt now in that brothel in Columbia Heights."

"And?"

"I told my friend Lourdes about you. Not by name, understand. And she told her girl Marisol. Marisol wants to speak to you. This dude Gustav is a real entrepreneur. Owns a house-painting business and a little jewelry store in Langley Park. Lourdes say it's one of those stores that never seems to have a customer in it."

"So Gustav is laundering cash through his other businesses."

"That's right."

"Is it okay if I contact Marisol?"

"She'll contact *you*. I'll give her your number if that's cool."

"It is."

"And if this pans out, there's something in it for me, right?"

"Something. Not a grand, though."

"You'll take care of me, Phil." Monique checked her watch and drained her wineglass. "You always been a gentleman."

* * *

ORNAZIAN SAT in his Edge in the neighborhood of Deanwood in Far Northeast, where brick apartment buildings mingled with houses in varying conditions on large lots. Deanwood's residents were urban in appearance but the atmosphere had a southern, country vibe. There were smokers and barbecue grills out in the yards, and men worked on their own cars here. Deanwood folks had been keeping chickens long before it became a suburban trend, and one man owned a goat. Ornazian was on the high ground, on Jay Street and Forty-Seventh. The hilly terrain with its view of the federal city was typical of D.C.'s eastern quadrants.

He was waiting for Christopher Perry, an attendee at the Weitzman party, to come back from school. Woodson High's day had ended a half an hour earlier and Ornazian was hoping to catch Perry as he arrived at his house, half of a ramshackle duplex that stood at the top of the hill. Ornazian knew a Woodson math teacher who had once been in a band, which was not an unusual progression for the Positive Force crowd. After assurances that Ornazian was not going to jam the kid up, the teacher had given him the name of the street on which Perry stayed, but he stopped short of giving him an address. A real property tax database search confirmed that a house on Jay Street was owned by a Debra Perry, Christopher's mother or grandmother.

Ornazian was about to give up and hit the ignition button when Christopher Perry appeared, walking east on Jay with a book bag slung over his shoulder. His face was an approximate match to the photo that appeared on his Facebook page.

Ornazian got out of his car and crossed the street. Perry, a big kid, eyed him mildly and without concern and kept walking. Ornazian was obviously off his turf. Deanwood and its adjacent neighborhood Burrville had yet to gentrify.

"Christopher Perry?" said Ornazian.

"Yeah?" Perry stopped walking and dropped his book bag, freeing his arms. It was what Ornazian would have done.

Ornazian had drawn his wallet and opened it to show Perry his license. "Phil Ornazian. I'm an investigator."

Unlike many who accepted the deliberately vague title of investigator, Perry studied the license before Ornazian closed his wallet.

"You're not MPD," said Perry.

"Private."

"So I don't have to talk to you."

"Let me ask you one question," said Ornazian. "You went to a party in Potomac, Maryland, recently."

"So?"

"The house got robbed of some valuable jewelry that night. A girl was sexually assaulted."

This caught his attention. He looked a bit surprised.

"You had a question?" said Perry.

"You know anything about that?" said Ornazian. "You were there with a friend, right?"

"Me and my boy had nothing to do with it."

"I didn't say you did. I'm just wondering if you saw anything. I'm working for the man who owns the house."

Perry shrugged. "We just went out there for fun. See if we could talk to some girls. Trust me, I wouldn't do it again."

"Why not?"

"Those people were acting *stupid*. Rich kids all trying to be like Gucci Mane and shit, sippin that Drank."

"You don't use it?"

"Nah, I don't mess with it. It'll do you permanent. Pimp C *died* behind it. Thing was, the kids at that party was *actin* more fucked up than they was."

"What are you talking about?"

"The dudes who brought the Lean, the ones who was sellin it? They were runnin a game."

"Who were they?"

"Three older white dudes, inked up. The guy I was with—"

"What's his name?"

"Nah. Uh-uh."

"Okay. Go on."

"My friend looked at one of the prescription bottles they brought in with them," said Perry. "They had taken a needle and syringed out some of the medicine. Probably replaced it with NyQuil or some shit like that."

"So they were cutting it. How do you know?"

"There was a burn mark on the bottle, where they had sealed the hole back up with fire. We know what that's about. But those kids out there in that fancy neighborhood don't know shit."

"Were these older guys the same ones who trashed the house?"

"Tellin you, I don't know. Me and my boy, we left out of there early."

"Why?"

"Those guys who brought the Lean were mean-muggin us. Calling us lawn jockeys and shit like that. Didn't care if we heard it either."

Ornazian considered that. It fit the profile, given what he had seen carved into the table at the Weitzman home.

"So you ghosted."

"We were outnumbered. Besides, I wanted to get back to a party I knew about in Northeast. Hang with my own."

Ornazian thought of his sons and what they would be facing in the world as they came of age. For a moment, he considered making an apology to Christopher Perry, even knowing how lame and ineffective it would be. But Perry had already picked up his book bag and was walking toward his home.

TWELVE

THE DISTRICT Line kitchen, in the basement, was not much bigger than the cooking area in most homes. It was L-shaped, and at the elbow of the L was a wood-fired oven where all of the prep and cooking was done. There was no grill. Beside the brick-faced oven was a steel rack holding split logs. Two separate stations, one for colds and salads, one for pizza toppings, were set up on each leg of the L, with refrigeration beneath the work boards. Beer and white wine were stored in a refrigerated walk-in, and there was shelving for canned goods and an area for kegs whose tap lines ran through the basement ceiling to the bar above. It was a crowded but efficiently organized space.

In another open space, around the corner from the kitchen's L, was the small station where Michael Hudson did his job. It too was very narrow and consisted of an automatic dishwasher and two stainless-steel basins with a power-spray nozzle and hose suspended above them. Mounted on the wall were chemical housing units with plastic tubing that automatically dispensed cleaning agents and nonspotting drying fluids to the dishwasher. The silverware, plates, and glassware went into the machine. The basins were used for the soaking and manual scrubbing of pots and pans.

When Michael was working at his station he stood grounded on rubber mats and wore an apron. To his left was an iron spiral staircase that led to the dining room. Food runners had to negotiate it, as did he when he delivered the racks of glassware to the bar. The steps were textured like manhole covers to minimize slippage. A person had to be careful and in fairly good shape to work here.

In the morning before opening and whenever else it was necessary, he went outside, split the logs of kiln-dried oak, brought bundles into the kitchen, and stacked them by the oven. The kitchen workers constantly fed the wood into the oven, which ran up to eight hundred degrees. They used long-handled peels to get pizzas, calzones, and roasted veggies in and out of the oven. Their inner forearms were frequently marked with burns.

Michael had figured out everything his first morning on the job. Didn't take a Rhodes Scholar to learn how to wash dishes, and that was the disappointing thing, at first. There was nothing really to look forward to; it was strange to realize that he wasn't going to have any more knowledge a year from now than he had acquired that very first day. But it was a paying job, and it was the routine he needed in his life.

The ladies in the kitchen, Maria and Blanca, were hard-working, devout Catholics and friendly to him despite the language barrier. He was cracking that pretty quickly too. He used *mucho, caliente, rapido, para qué,* and *gracias, señora* and sometimes *señorita* if he was being innocently flattering. They called him Miguel and "baby," and he called them *mamacita* and "mommy." They were in their twenties, had children, and already looked middle-aged, but they had light in their eyes and in their smiles.

The men who worked the kitchen were less friendly but not aggressively so. Maybe they had been tight with the man whom Michael had replaced. Befriending them would take more time. But Michael had made headway there too. One of the men, Joe, would greet Michael in a boxer's stance and throw soft combinations at him as he passed. That was his idea of an olive branch. They called Michael *el hombre alto*. He towered over all of them.

On day and night shifts, the kitchen workers played their Spanish music through a Bluetooth speaker set up near the colds station. To Michael it sounded like he was at a party or a carnival all the time. After a day he tired of it and began to use earbuds to listen to his own stuff, a little go-go and hip-hop but mainly the R & B he had heard his mother play while he was growing up in her house. He could have listened to novels that way too, but he found he didn't care for the experience. He didn't read e-books either. To him, a book was like a painting that hung in a museum. It was like a piece of art. There was nothing that compared to holding a book in his hands and scanning the words on the page. It made him "see" what he was reading. It was how he dreamed.

So he brought a book with him to work every day. Read it at lunch up in the empty dining room on the third floor or sitting at one of the picnic tables on the patio if it was nice outside. Sometimes Angelos Valis would join him, just for a few minutes, not to bother him but to ask him how things were going.

"Why they call this place the District Line?" said Michael. "We're five, six miles away from Mer'land."

"The owner's father remembers a column called the District Line that ran every day in the *Washington Post*. A guy named Bill Gold wrote it."

"When dinosaurs roamed the earth."

"There's another local restaurant with the same name, in a hotel. They don't bother us about it."

"Y'all should change the name."

"What would *you* name this place if you had the chance?"

"Michael Hudson's."

"Of course." Angelos smiled. "I'll see if I can get the sign changed today."

At the end of those conversations, Michael always thanked Angelos for the opportunity he had given him. He meant it too.

SINCE HIS interview with Christopher Perry, Phil Ornazian had attempted to reach out to several of the kids who'd attended the Weitzman party, with little response. Most of them had ignored the messages he'd sent through Facebook, and those who had hit him back told him they had no interest in speaking with him. Finally, a girl named Britany, a friend of Lisa's, said that she'd meet with him somewhere that was not her home.

He got up with Britany after school one day at the food court in Montgomery Mall. He bought her some food at Cava, a fast-casual Mediterranean spot, and as she ate, he asked her questions. She claimed she didn't know who had robbed the Weitzman home or who had assaulted Lisa. Her eyes and body language told Ornazian that these assertions were lies. He found her both dishonest and vacuous and wondered why she was here beyond a free lunch. But when she easily gave up the name of a boy who had been at the party, along with his home address, Ornazian realized why she'd agreed to speak with him. Britany wanted to point him toward someone with whom she had had a relationship that was now a personal beef. From the way she talked about him, he could sense that she was angry at the kid and was also still into him. He was a boy who'd done her wrong.

His name was Billy Hanrahan. He went to a private school in Potomac, which was good for Ornazian. She said that Billy had recognized one of the older guys who'd crashed the party. So the meeting with Britany, which had seemed worthless at first, had turned up gold.

As Britany finished off her meal, Ornazian got a text from Marisol, the woman who worked at the brothel in Columbia Heights. She would see him but had only a small window in which to do so, and it was now.

"I've got to go," said Ornazian.

"Don't give me up," said Britany.

Ornazian left her there and drove back into town.

MARISOL HAD texted him a photo, so Ornazian knew who he was looking for, and he found her seated alone at Compass Coffee on Seventh Street, in Shaw. She was an attractive girl in her early twenties, wearing an inexpensive, low-cut dress beneath a spring coat. Her eyes were almond-shaped and very dark, as were her eyebrows. He surmised her hair was naturally black, but today it was reddish from a rinse. She had the features of a native Guatemalan.

After he introduced himself, he bought them two coffees, returned to the wood-laminate table, and sat down. She was nervous as a cat, looking around and out the plate-glass window that fronted the store. He spoke softly in an attempt to put her at ease.

"I'm going to take some notes," said Ornazian, opening the Moleskine notebook with lined paper that he carried with him. "For me only. No one else will ever see them. Okay?"

"Yes, Mr. Ornay-jun."

"Call me Phil."

"Phil."

"Where do you work?"

She told him. It was a row house on a mostly residential street in Columbia Heights, just inside Georgia Avenue, northwest of Howard U.

"Describe the layout," said Ornazian.

"There is a bar and place to sit on the first floor where we present ourselves. Four small rooms upstairs where we work."

"Security?"

"A couple of men, always. And Gustavo and his man, when they come."

"His man?"

"Cesar. His *segundo* and bodyguard. Gustavo has a business down the street. Little more than a bar and a pool table. Is called the Nine Ball."

"He comes to collect the money?"

"He comes to do whatever he wants. Sometimes he comes to pay others."

"What others?"

"For protection. The MS-Thirteen."

"They're in the brothel all the time?"

"Only to pick up their money. Twice a week."

"Is there a lot of money coming in and going out?"

Marisol shrugged. "I don't see the money. But I think so."

"What do you mean, you don't see the money?"

"I don't touch it. Some of the other girls keep half of what they make, after they've paid the house for condoms and wipes. I'm working off my entry to this country. I keep nothing. Sometimes I get tips."

"Where does the money go?"

"Gustavo and Cesar take the money out in a leather briefcase at the end of every night. On the weekends there are two briefcases."

"Take it out where?"

"I don't know." Marisol reached into a small handbag and produced a slip of paper. "But here is where Gustavo lives."

Ornazian took the paper and scanned a Hyattsville, Maryland, address. "You've been here?"

"For his parties."

"Why did you write his address down?"

"Because I hoped this day would come."

"What do you want?" said Ornazian.

"Money," said Marisol. "For me and my baby girl. I have a brother in Houston. He works the construction. I will go to him."

Ornazian thought it over. "It would be good for me to get a look inside that brothel."

She shook her head. "You cannot come in. No gringos."

"What if I send a Hispanic man in?"

"Only El Salvadorans. If a Mexican or a Nicaraguan comes in, they know it is some kind of police."

"So where do the customers come from?"

"They find them at bus stops. Or the spots where the men wait for work. Home Depot. Seven-Eleven. They bring them to the house in vans. Even a man who is out of work can find thirty dollars if he is lonely for a woman."

"You speak good English."

"I lived near the embassy in Guatemala City from when I was young. I cleaned apartments. There were many Americans." Marisol looked around once again and leaned in close to Ornazian. "No one can ever know we spoke."

"You can trust me."

"I'm afraid." She bit her lip. Shyly she said, "What will I get?"

"A thousand dollars. Clear the message you texted me along with your photo. Clear out my contact information from your phone. From here on in, I'll reach out to you if I need you."

"So you will help me."

Ornazian said, "I need to think it over."

But in his head he said *Yes*.

THIRTEEN

ANNA AND Rick Byrne had wanted to get some dinner out and maybe a drink after their meal, so they walked over to the strip on Eleventh Street, where there were choices. Rick was in the mood for one of those wood-oven pizzas they made at the District Line, and Anna, who liked the food there, was fine with that. The plan was dinner at the DL, then maybe a beer afterward at Wonderland or Meridian Pint. They had done this very same thing many times before.

At the restaurant, they sat at the bar, their preference. The ginger-haired tender set them up with silverware and they ordered two personal-size pizzas and a couple of D.C. Brau pale ales. Anna had her hair down and was wearing mostly black and a pair of distressed short Frye boots. Rick was wearing his gear: track pants, a white pullover sporting the Callaway logo, and gray New Balance 990s. To strangers, they appeared to be a couple going in two different directions, and that assumption was not incorrect. Rick's trajectory was toward a retirement golf community in Florida, where the people looked like him, had five-thirty cocktails and early-bird specials. Anna preferred to live out her life in a city where there was diversity and culture. But this was undiscussed because it was so far away.

The place was busy, but no one was in the weeds. The bartender was playing a long jam over the house stereo. It sounded like African music, and Rick said, "Who is this, Paul Simon?" and the bartender said, "Fela Kuti."

"Paul Simon," said Anna, and chuckled.

"What?" said Rick.

He talked to her about a corporate case he was involved with. Something to do with insider trading. He might have to travel down to Atlanta soon to take a deposition. She kept the conversation going politely. She *was* interested in what he was up to, but her mind had wandered to her book club, which was coming up in the chapel that week. She had chosen a literary novel for the men, and she wondered if she had erred, as the book was very well written but light on plot. Also, she was second-guessing the mostly nonfiction books she had staged that afternoon for the GED unit and that she was set to deliver the next morning.

She was staring off, thinking on her job, when Michael Hudson appeared at the service end of the bar, a rack of glassware in his arms. He was wearing a watch cap and an apron over a T-shirt, and his face was sheened with sweat. He placed the glassware rack on the bar and looked out into the dining room. He saw Anna and smiled. She felt herself smile back with spontaneous affection. So Michael was out in the world, working. He hadn't transitioned to a federal prison.

Michael grabbed what looked like a clean bar rag, wiped his face dry, and walked down to where Anna and her companion were seated.

"Michael," she said, taking his hand and shaking it firmly.

"Miss Anna."

"Just Anna, please."

"Okay. Anna."

"This is my husband, Rick."

Rick, a gentleman and a fan of ritual, got off his stool to shake Michael's hand. They were both tall men.

"Nice to meet you," said Rick, and then he looked to Anna for an explanation.

"Michael was one of my clients."

"Anna turned me on to books," said Michael.

"Cool," said Rick, and he sat back down.

"So, you're working here," said Anna lamely.

"Yeah, I'm down in the kitchen. Been here since I got out."

"I didn't know what happened to you."

"My charges got dropped," said Michael. "I'm not on parole. Just, you know, *done*. So it's all good, you know?"

"I'll say. Congratulations."

"I been reading. Got a library card and everything. Bought a couple of those books you turned me on to so I can start my own collection. I'm staying at my mother's house over on Sherman."

"We don't live far from here either. We're in Park View."

Anna could feel Rick's eyes on her and she decided to say no more. She was just making conversation but she knew her husband would find it odd that she'd give out such information to an offender. She barely knew Michael but she trusted him.

They all felt the silence.

"I better get back to it," said Michael, adjusting the watch cap he wore jauntily cocked on his head. "The dishes are backin up. You got any recommendations for me?"

"We're reading *The Beautiful Things That Heaven Bears* in the book club. It's by a young Ethiopian writer, set in D.C. I think you might like it."

"Beautiful Things That Heaven Bears," said Michael, repeating the title like he used to do when Anna would give him verbal tips in lockup. "I'll check it out. Thanks, Anna."

"You're very welcome," said Anna.

"Nice to meet you," said Michael to Rick, and once more he shook his hand.

"You too," said Rick.

Michael went back toward the hallway. He glanced over his shoulder and met Anna's gaze one more time, then entered the hall and descended the staircase. When she'd looked into his eyes, Anna felt something stir inside her, and it confused her. Rick's voice nearly startled her.

"What was that about?" said Rick.

"He's a good guy."

"He's a criminal. And you told him where we lived."

"I identified our neighborhood, that's all. He doesn't even know our last name. I go by Anna Kaplan in the jail, remember? Besides, Michael would never bother me."

Rick shook his head. "Don't be so naive, Anna."

Maybe she was naive. But she thought Michael Hudson was one of the good guys, and she was happy for him. It seemed like he was doing fine.

Later, after the restaurant had closed, Michael approached the bartender, Callie, who was using the soda gun to rinse out her nets and asked her if he could have a look at the credit card receipts from the night. It was probably against the rules, but Callie liked Michael and she let him do it.

* * *

AFTER MIDNIGHT, Ornazian and Thaddeus Ward sat on a street off Georgia Avenue in Columbia Heights, near a bar that was identified solely by an illustration of a nine ball on a light box. Its plate-glass window had been tinted nearly black and the window was mostly covered with posters advertising twenty-dollar buckets of Corona and single bottles of limed-up Bud Lights for two seventy-five. The writing on the posters was in Spanish and there were small-statured men going in and out of the spot and some who stood outside the door catching smokes. There was a video camera mounted above the door.

Ornazian and Ward were in a Lincoln Mark, one of Ward's black cars. They were parked tightly behind an SUV that was blocking a view of their front license plate. Down the street toward Georgia, a half a block away, stood a simple, unremarkable row house. A preteen boy sat in a chair beside the front steps, cell phone in hand. Above the front door was a short pole holding a rolled-up flag. A video camera was mounted on the brick wall over a second-floor window.

"Lotta cameras on this block," said Ward.

"Lot of cameras everywhere," said Ornazian. "Takes the sport out of the game."

A white windowless van pulled up in front of the house. The boy got on his cell and spoke into it, and then five Hispanic men got out of the van and entered the house.

"That lookout kid just talked to someone inside," said Ward. "And I'll bet if that flag is unfurled, it's some kind of sign too. Like, 'We got lawmen on the premises, don't come in.' They got this shit wired up tight. You said they using MS-Thirteen for security?"

"They call it security. But I think it's the opposite. It's payoff money to keep MS-Thirteen off their backs."

"You reckon our boy Gustav got his own men in there with iron?"

"I would think. But we're not going to take him off in the whorehouse."

"Would be good to get a look inside it."

"They don't let anyone in but El Salvadorans."

"Remember my employee Esteban?" said Ward. "You met him. He's from that neck of the woods."

"Esteban is Spanish for Stephen."

"For real?"

"I'm sure he's a nice guy, good school spirit and all that. But we don't need Esteban."

"You mean you don't want to cut him in."

"That too."

"We could darken you up some and send you in. But then you might have to partake. And I know you wouldn't do that. 'Cause you're—what's that word? *Monogamous*."

"It's from the Greek. *Monos* means 'alone.' *Gamos* means 'marriage.' But *gamo* is also the Greek vulgar for 'fucking.' So *monogamous* means 'one fuck.' If you want to get deep about it."

"You call that deep?"

Ornazian got into the photos in his iPhone and found what he was looking for. He handed the phone to Ward. "Here. That's why I don't stray."

Ward looked at the photo. It was Ornazian's wife, Sydney, lying nude on their bed in a provocative pose.

"Damn, boy. She's finer than a motherfucker. How did an ugly-lookin dude like you hook up with that?"

"I'm like a can of Coke down there."

"You mean when you shake it, it pops off."

"Funny."

Ward handed Ornazian the phone.

Soon three men walked out of the Nine Ball and headed down the block toward the brothel. A swaggering overweight man with a cat mustache, wearing an ill-fitting sport jacket and a thick tie, was clearly the leader. Another man, short of stature, built, with the clean-shaven face of a native Central American, walked beside him. A third man, predictably goateed and with gelled hair, trailed them.

"The fat man would be Gustav," said Ornazian.

"So that Wladislaw-lookin cat next to him would be his top gun."

"Wladislaw?"

"Charles Bronson in *The Dirty Dozen*. Like everything I speak on, it's before your time."

"If that's Gustav's *segundo*, his name is Cesar."

The men entered the brothel.

"We're gonna need a driver," said Ornazian.

"This does look a little more complicated than our usual thing," said Ward. "You got someone in mind?"

"Yeah. There's a guy who owes me a favor. Stand-up dude, can handle a car."

"How do you know him?"

"He was up on felony charges and was looking at five years. Pulled a rip-and-run on a marijuana dealer."

"And?"

"The dealer called 911 on my man and his partner as soon as they robbed him."

"That's against the code."

"You'd think. Police arrived on the scene and gave chase as he and his partner were pulling away. My man lost them but they made his plates. He was driving his mother's car."

"That's not smart."

"I think he's aware of that now. When he was arrested, he refused to give up his partner. My man took the gun charge even though he told me he never touched one."

"And why does he owe you?"

"I got him off."

"How'd you do that?"

"I found the marijuana dealer and told him that he needed to think very carefully of the health and welfare of his family."

"In so many words, you threatened his wife and kids."

"Semantics. I would never have done anything to his spouse or his children. You know that. The point is, he made the right decision and opted not to testify."

"And you did this why? Sayin, what was the reasoning behind you sticking your neck way out for this driver?"

"I was banking a favor. The way things are for you and me, we got a little business going now. Like any business, we're gonna grow. The jobs get more complex, we're gonna need help. I knew this dude could handle a car. And I saw that he would stand tall if he got under the hot lights. What I'm telling you is, he was a find. I knew I could use him up the road."

"Huh," said Ward.

"What's that mean?"

"Witness tampering. You could get a dime for that. When's the last time you took a job and did it clean?"

"It's a war out here," said Ornazian. "I'm trying to feed my family."

"I been in a war, young man. This ain't it."

"Feels that way to me."

"The more you cross the line, the harder it is to come back. Believe me, I know."

"Let me worry about that."

Gustav, Cesar, and the third man came out of the brothel and went toward a black Range Rover Sport that was parked across the street. Cesar was carrying a leather briefcase. He got behind the wheel and Gustav took the passenger seat. The third man got into a blue Mustang GT and cooked the ignition. The SUV started and pulled off the curb. The driver of the Mustang followed.

Ward ignitioned the Lincoln, waited, then followed the Range Rover north on Georgia.

"Keep it loose," said Ornazian. "I don't care if we lose them. I have his home address. He lives out in Hyattsville. I want to see if he makes any stops before he goes to his house."

Ward side-glanced Ornazian. "Can I see your phone again? I just want to look at something."

Ornazian ignored this and settled into his seat.

Gustav and his men did not stop. They went directly to his house. Ornazian and Ward surveilled the residence and talked about a plan.

FOURTEEN

ONE DAY, walking home from work, Michael Hudson saw an unfinished, three-level, freestanding bookcase that had been placed out on the curb in front of a restored row home on Sherman Ave. It had a piece of notepaper taped to it and on the paper, written in black Magic Marker, was the word Free. Michael guessed it had been put out by one of the new residents in the neighborhood. Those folks tended to throw things away before it was time.

Michael inspected the unit. It was a piece from Ikea or someplace like it, fitted together with barrel dowels. He knuckled one of the shelves. Felt like wood and not particleboard. He lifted up the bookcase and carried it away.

A couple of blocks from his mother's house, he came up on Carla Thomas, who was on the porch of her grandmother's place with her daughter, Alisha. Carla called his name. Michael put the bookcase down and walked up the steps to her porch.

"Hey, Michael."

"How you doin, Carla? Hi, baby girl."

"Hi," said Alisha shyly.

"Thought you were gonna come past," said Carla.

"So you been thinking of me."

"A little." She pointed her chin down to the sidewalk. "What you doing with that piece of furniture?"

"It's to hold books. I'm gonna fix it up and put it in my room."

"You read books?" she said, rather suspiciously.

"Yeah. You?"

"I don't have the time."

"Look here." Michael produced his cell. "I got a phone now so maybe we should, you know, trade digits."

"Okay."

Michael and Carla exchanged phones and entered their numbers. Michael took his back.

"Maybe I'll hit you up," he said.

"Maybe?"

"I *will.*"

"Can I get my cell back?"

Michael stepped closer and handed Carla her phone, and as he did, he took in her sweet scent, whatever she was wearing, perfume or oils or whatnot. She smelled like strawberries. It was nice.

"I'm going to school next year," said Alisha, who had been left out of the conversation.

"I bet you're smart," said Michael. He squinted. "You got something on your face, Alisha."

He reached down and playfully flicked her cheek. She rubbed at the spot. It stung just a little but she liked the attention.

"Don't forget," said Carla.

Michael nodded and said good-bye to them both. He picked up his bookcase and walked south.

UP WHERE he slept, in the bedroom he'd shared with his older brother, Thomas, when they'd come up, Michael placed the bookcase against the wall beside his dresser, where there was a space. There were some rough spots in the wood, some splintering along the edges, and the connections were shaky where they had been joined by the little dowel rods. Michael would fix that permanently with wood glue and C-clamps. He intended to sand and stain the shelves as well.

He put the two Elmore Leonard Western books he owned on one of the shelves, spines out like they did at the library, so he could read the titles. And then, just to see how it looked, he shelved a couple of library books the same way. He intended to fill this bookcase, and when there was no more space he would buy another set of shelves, maybe even one of those old-time ones that had hinged glass doors. Once he got himself situated with some pocket money, that is. All in good time.

On the other half of the room was his brother's twin bed and his dresser, crowded with all the trophies Thomas had earned, from Pop Warner through high school. Michael's mother dusted them regularly. Not that she was holding the room as some kind of shrine. She kept a clean house. Even had those plastic runners on the carpet downstairs.

It was said that most parents had favorites, but Michael felt his mother loved all three of her kids equally. Thomas had been the athlete, the straight one, right into the military out of high school, and he had his life insurance, health insurance, and pension already in place. Olivia was the smart one who'd applied herself, taken the right AP classes, bolstered her résumé with after-school activities, and went after that minority scholarship money on her own. She said she was going to go into public relations, but whatever she did, he had no doubt it would be big.

Michael had struggled, obviously, but outsiders would never know it if they spoke to his mom. She had stuck with him, even that last time, when he'd used her car to do the robbery. Sometimes he felt like he'd never atone for that. Sure, his boy Mario had talked him into it, but Michael could have said no. He had done the dirt at a time in his life when he felt he had no worth. After he'd lost that thing at the Foot Locker. And then been let go from the Best Buy. Once again without a job, out of money, and low on self-esteem. For the wrong minute Mario's plan to take off the weed dealer had made sense. It seemed like a solution when all along it was a trap. It also sounded exciting and a little dangerous, and those were sensations that Michael had always chased too. But the person he had been was standing far behind him now. All he could do going forward was try to be right.

His mother called his name from downstairs.

THEY ATE dinner, a Peruvian chicken his mother had brought home from one of those amigo storefronts in Columbia Heights, at the dining-room table. Doretha Hudson was drinking her glass of wine, the only one she'd take all day, and Michael was having ice water. He'd never liked the taste of alcohol or how it made him feel. His mother had said a prayer before dinner and Michael had bowed his head along with her, though he was far from sure. He was being respectful to his mom.

Brandy was lying across one of Michael's bare feet and snoring. Occasionally Michael would wiggle his toes to play with the dog, but Brandy didn't stir.

"This dog got one paw in the grave," said Michael.

"Don't say that," said his mother, looking as if a shudder had gone through her. She was silent for a minute, then said, "Everything good, Michael? Your job?"

"Good for now."

"When you were little…" said Doretha.

"Yeah?" Michael thought he knew what was coming, but he didn't stop her. She'd earned the right to lecture him.

"You were exceptional. Smart and funny. My friends called you 'the magic baby' 'cause you caught on to things so quick. You could imitate folks…I remember when you got up on-stage in the third grade and did that 'Jiggy with It' song. You sounded just like Will did on the record. You weren't nervous at all."

"When you're young, you got no fear. I didn't know enough to be scared."

"I thought you'd…"

"What? Grow up to be something special?"

"I didn't mean that, exactly."

"It's not like I planned this," said Michael.

It was true. His head got turned around without him even realizing it when he'd hit his early teens. Got to be that his friends had more influence on him than his mother. Three boys in particular he ran with. Two of them, Junior and David, grew up and out of that mind-set and now were doing all right, more or less. And then there was Mario. Mario hadn't changed.

If his mother only knew the stuff he was into at an early age. He'd had sex with a girl when he was eleven, the kind of neighborhood gal who liked to get with boys who were inexperienced. Soon after, at twelve or thirteen, the bad started. The usual trouble that some young men find. Stealing things you didn't need from stores and unlocked cars. Fights. That swell of adrenaline when you stepped to someone. Sometimes he was the aggressor and sometimes not. Most confrontations you couldn't walk away from 'less you wanted to be labeled a punk. Which got him suspended from school a couple of times. Put him in a cycle.

Next there was joyriding. This led him to hotwiring cars. He was a natural under the wheel. He could handle the hell out of a vehicle; he just took to it right away. Liked to drive fast too. Until he got caught for the second time. Got sent to Oak Hill and a six-by-nine cell, a cot and mattress on a concrete floor. Mice and roaches running over him at night. More fights. A guard who swung on him, and he swung back. They put him on meds after that, made him dead inside. When he came out, harder than before, he stole another car.

Looking back, he couldn't see any reason to it. Just impulse and confusion. Wasn't like that for all young men, but for some, it was. The brain did change eventually. For many, put into the system and damaged by it, that change came too late.

But this last thing, this rip-and-run with Mario? A man his age? He had no excuse for that.

"I'm just saying that I had high hopes for you," said Doretha.

"Had?"

"You didn't let me finish. I still do."

"Thank you, Mama."

"Just keep doing what you're doing."

"I will."

"Small steps," said Doretha.

"Yes, ma'am."

THE CLOCKS had sprung forward, and it was still light out, so Michael sat on the rocker couch out on the porch and read his latest library book, *The Beautiful Things That Heaven Bears*. It was the novel Anna had recommended the night she and her husband had come into the DL. Took some concentration to get into it, and careful reading, but he was glad he had given it a try. All these African immigrants throughout the city and inner suburbs, working in parking garages, owning small businesses, coffeehouses and the like, and Michael had never really thought too much about them or what was going on in their heads. Until he'd read this book. What would Anna have said if she were leading the book club? It was "a window into their inner lives."

A car horn sounded on Sherman Ave. Michael looked down to the street. There, in an idling, midsize black SUV, sat Phil Ornazian, the private detective who had worked Michael's case.

Michael had not thought much about the reason for the unexpected dropping of his charges. More to the point, he had kept it from his mind.

He put the book down on the rocker couch, stood, and walked down the concrete steps to the street.

"**HOW'S IT** going?" said Ornazian.

"I'm at a restaurant on Eleventh. The District Line. Kitchen job. It's steady."

"Glad it's working out for you."

"Never got a chance to thank you for what you did to get me off," said Michael. "For whatever you did."

Ornazian said, "The thank-you part comes now."

They were seated in the front buckets of the Edge. Ornazian had his satellite radio on and he was keeping the music low. The display screen said they were listening to a song from something called Run the Jewels, an act Michael did not know. He wondered if Ornazian was playing hip-hop on Michael's account or if he listened to it for pleasure on his own.

"How'd you do it?" said Michael. "They had me airtight."

"I knew I could change the man's mind for the same reason you knew you could take him off. He was a boy playing a man's game. White private-school kid from Ward Three, college grad. Moves over to Shaw and all of a sudden he thinks he's street. Thinks he can apply his business degree to marijuana distribution. Lead a normal life, a wife and two kids, a house off Seventh Street, while he does his thing. After all, it's just marijuana. But dealing weed's the same as selling heroin or coke. It's a prop in the underground economy, which means hard people are involved and they will try to take what you've got. Which is why you and your boy pulled the rip-and-run on him. Right?"

"Didn't work out so good for me."

"You thought the man had a code. Some people who were born privileged act like it the rest of their lives. He was outraged that you would rob him. He was more than ready to put you away."

"And what stopped him?"

"I convinced him not to testify."

"How?"

"It doesn't matter, does it? What matters is, you dodged five years in a federal joint."

"And now's the thank-you part."

Ornazian nodded. "I'm about to rob a man who has a brothel in Columbia Heights. We're going to take him off at his house in Hyattsville. Me and an associate of mine. An ex-cop."

"So you're doing a home invasion."

"We're gonna relieve a slave trader of his ill-gotten gains."

"That's how you sellin it to yourself?"

"He's a bad guy."

"I'm not participating in no robbery."

"You won't be in the house. You won't touch a weapon. But there are too many variables for us to handle the thing ourselves. I need a driver."

"Get someone else."

"I know you can drive. You dusted the police the night you pulled the robbery. And I know I can trust you. You never gave up your associate. You stood tall."

"Get someone else."

Ornazian sighed. Michael couldn't tell if he really was regretful or if it was all a show.

"You know, Michael…"

"*What?*"

"The judge dismissed your case without prejudice. That means you could be retried. That is, if the witness changes his mind and decides to testify."

"You'd set that in motion?"

"I wouldn't like it."

"What about you? What if I talked about what you did? Witness tampering draws serious time."

"Then I guess we'd both be fucked. But you won't do that, Michael. You're doing well out here. You don't want to mess with that now."

Michael said nothing. Their windows were down, and both of them let the proposition settle as they listened to the radio and the car sounds in the street.

"I don't know what the take will be," said Ornazian. "But I'll guarantee you a thousand dollars for two, three hours of work. It could be more."

Michael did not respond.

"I'll get you a car," said Ornazian. "I'll find you something fast."

Again, there was no response. Ornazian asked for Michael's new cell number and Michael gave it up. Then Ornazian took Michael's cell and entered his own number into the phone. Michael pulled the latch on his door, telling Ornazian that their conversation was over.

"I'll be in touch," said Ornazian.

Michael walked up the steps to his mother's house.

Ornazian pulled off the curb and headed north, toward Petworth. Sydney had phoned him about dinner. She was cooking a fish stew.

FIFTEEN

BILLY HANRAHAN attended a prep school in Potomac that, in Ornazian's day, had had a reputation as a military-style academy where parents sent their sons for structure and discipline. The school was now co-ed and its rep as a place for wayward boys had changed. Billy lived in the school district of Walt Whitman High, among the highest-achieving public schools in the country, so there had to be a reason that Billy's parents were spending forty thousand dollars a year on private-school tuition. Maybe Billy needed a competitive environment and a focus on academics and achievement. Maybe his parents liked their friends to see the school's coat-of-arms decal on the back window of their luxury car. The reason was immaterial, but the lives of the wealthy were endlessly fascinating to Ornazian.

The afternoon after he spoke to Michael Hudson, Ornazian was parked on a block of nice but unspectacular homes on a residential street in Bethesda, between River Road and Bradley Boulevard, waiting for Billy to return home from school. Ornazian had used Billy's Facebook page, which identified the father, and the people-finder program to find the Hanrahans' address. Billy was a senior, and if tradition in this zip code was intact, he would have his own car, most likely a model that was highly rated for safety and had been handed down or purchased used. Sure enough, twenty minutes after school let out, a ten-year-old ruby-red Volvo XC90 with aftermarket roof bars rolled down the block and stopped in front of the Hanrahan house.

Ornazian got out of his car at the same time Billy did. Billy was solidly built, average height, with wavy black hair that just touched his collar. He wore a navy blazer, Dockers khakis, a white shirt, and the school's rep tie, loosely knotted. Like Christopher Perry, he carried a book bag on his shoulder. As Ornazian approached him, he stood straight and puffed up his chest.

"Can I speak to you for a minute?"

"What for?"

Ornazian pulled his wallet and flashed his license. "I'm an investigator."

"I **WAS** there," said Billy.

"Good," said Ornazian. "That's a start."

They were tight against the Volvo, standing in the street. Billy glanced over his shoulder at the bay window that fronted his house. Ornazian wondered if one or both of his parents were home. There was a black BMW X5 parked in the driveway.

"I won't keep you long," said Ornazian. "Answer my questions and you can go inside."

"I can go inside right now."

Ornazian looked him over. He was handsome, and aware of it, with a lock of hair that was carefully styled to hang over his forehead. He cocked an eyebrow when he spoke. He knew where the camera was at all times.

"Is that your mom's BMW?"

"Yeah?"

"Maybe I'll go in with you and we can all talk together."

"I've already spoken with my mom and dad. I told them what happened at the party. They know I wasn't involved."

"So you covered yourself."

"I didn't do anything wrong."

"Do your parents know that you didn't step in and help that girl when she was being assaulted?"

Billy looked away. "I wasn't in that room."

"I have it on good authority that you knew one of the guys who assaulted the girl."

"Who told you that?" Ornazian didn't answer and Billy said, "Britany?"

"Never mind who."

"That little trick."

"Easy, Billy. That's not nice. Now, I'm pretty sure the ones who assaulted Lisa are the same ones who trashed the house and robbed it. And don't say it was those black guys who came up from D.C., because I know that's not true."

"I'm not sayin *anything*. You're not with the police and I don't have to speak to you."

"That's true."

"My father told me that if anyone tried to question me about the party, I should tell them they should speak with our lawyer."

Billy began to walk away.

"Where you going to school next year, Billy?" This stopped the kid in his tracks. "You're a senior, right? I know you must be going on to college."

"So?"

"Your prep school has a code of conduct. I downloaded it right off their website. Your parents might not be too concerned about what happened that night, but I'm guessing your headmaster might. All the drinking and drugs. The robbery. The rape of a sixteen-year-old girl. Your presence there, and the fact that you didn't step in to try and stop it or report it to the police…it could very well affect your future."

"What the *fuck*."

"Tell me what you know and I won't bring this to your school."

"You'd do that?"

"I wouldn't take any pleasure in it. But, yes, I would."

Billy lowered his gaze. "Okay. I recognized one of those guys."

"I can't hear you."

Billy looked up, anger flaring in his eyes. "Can you hear me now?"

"Yes."

"I have a friend at school I'm pretty tight with. Brian Kelly. He's got an older brother named Terrance. Goes by Terry. He was one of them."

"Did you speak to him that night?"

"No."

"Tell me about him."

"All I know is what Brian's told me. Terry's, like, twenty-three now. When he went to our school he was a pretty good baseball player. Real good. He could hit and he had a hot glove. Second baseman. He was D-One material but he fucked it up."

"How?"

"Started hanging out with guys on the east side of Montgomery County. He was one of those kids who was always trying to act black. You know, like he thought he was gangsta."

"That's black?"

"*You* know what I'm saying. He got caught up in it, nearly failed out his senior year. Then he got busted on a distribution charge, lost his scholarship money, his college acceptance, everything."

"Marijuana?"

Billy nodded. "He flipped on his friends to get off. After, he started getting messages on his cell about what happens to snitches. Word was Terry got scared 'cause he thought those kids in Silver Spring, out Cherry Hill Road way, were gonna smoke him. All of a sudden he wasn't so black anymore. Basically, he got punked out. That's when he changed."

"Changed how?"

"He went the other way. Like, *all* the way. He hooked up with these guys who hated on black people, Muslims, Mexicans…shit like that."

"White supremacists."

"That's what his brother says. Terry's head got turned around. He's all fucked up."

"Were those the guys he was with that night?"

"I guess so. They had those fashy haircuts. Ink."

"Hipsters wear their hair that way too. And you been to the beach lately? *Grandmothers* have ink."

"All right, it was those *kinda* guys. He was with them. Okay?"

"Does Terry stay with his parents?"

"Brian says he's in and out."

"Terry has a car?"

"He drives a Charger his father bought him, back when he was doing good in school."

"Where does the Kelly family live?"

"Over in Glen Echo Heights, off MacArthur Boulevard. Wagner Lane."

"You got an address?"

"I never looked at the numbers on the house."

"Okay."

"Is that all?"

"You can go."

But Billy didn't move. His face had reddened and his right fist was clenched. Ornazian wondered if Billy was going to swing on him. It was plain that he wanted to.

"I said you can go," said Ornazian.

"Who *are* you?"

Ornazian left him there and walked back to his Ford.

SIXTEEN

LATE IN the afternoon, Anna staged the next morning's mobile library carts down in the workroom as her assistant, Carmia, checked in books and inspected them for contraband. Earlier that day, Anna had serviced the Fifty and Older unit. The men there, who had not outgrown their troubles, had tastes and sensibilities going back to their childhoods. Sidney Sheldon was very popular, as were Ernest Tidyman's Shaft novels, Chester Himes's Coffin Ed and Grave Digger Jones books, the street pulp of Donald Goines, and the potboilers of bestselling author Harold Robbins. *The Carpetbaggers,* a novel that was a thinly veiled version of Howard Hughes's life, featured a character named Nevada Smith and spawned the cult Steve McQueen Western of the same name. It was an inmate favorite. The lead character in the book was a man called Jonas Cord, referred to with admiration as a "cock star" by the men. Many of the inmates had read the dirty parts of the novel, filched off their fathers' or mothers' nightstands, when they were kids. The carnal scenes in Robbins's books were discussed with an almost academic intricacy, though nothing that approached the reverence surrounding that most hallowed sex passage in popular fiction, the one involving a bridesmaid, Sonny Corleone, and his "enormous, blood-gorged pole of muscle," commonly referred to around the jail as "Page 28."

When Anna was on this ward, she was inevitably reminded of an inmate named Lester Irby, a writer who'd had an entry, "God Don't Like Ugly," in a short-story collection set in the District that had been distributed by a legit New York publisher. Irby, seventy, had died of a stroke while incarcerated in the D.C. Jail. The unit got swelteringly hot during the summer months, and it was said that faulty air-conditioning ducts prevented cool air from reaching the block. The heat, most likely, contributed to his death. Anna missed Mr. Irby still. With her, he had always been a gentleman.

"Anna, you ready?" said Carmia. "I got to pick up my baby."

"Yes. Let's go."

THAT EVENING, Anna suggested to Rick that they have dinner at the District Line, and Rick said, "What, you wanna go see your boyfriend?"

Anna didn't smile or defend herself, so he didn't push the joke. She didn't like it when he kidded her about the offenders she knew or cracked on her job. Since he had moved up in the law firm, Rick had become a little cynical about people who committed crimes or, in general, those who led imperfect lives. He talked about the choices people made, as if everyone came from the same starting point or was lucky enough to have drawn the inside lane by an accident of birth. But then, when she became annoyed, she checked herself, because she lived with Rick and she knew who he was. Despite his sometimes sarcastic words, he was a decent man in his everyday inter-actions. She watched the courtesy he showed their neighbors and listened to how he dealt with people who worked in the restaurants and bars they frequented. He never talked down to anyone. Rick was becoming more of a law-and-order man as he grew older, which was not uncommon, and he was also basically good.

"We can go somewhere else if you want to," said Anna. "But you always talk about how you like the food and the atmo-sphere there."

"The DL is fine."

They sat out on the patio, lit by strings of Christmas lights, because it was warm enough and the night sky was clear. They were at a table along the sidewalk. Anna had placed her cell phone on the table's edge and they were drinking a couple of beers, sharing a prosciutto and gorgonzola bruschetta, and waiting for their pizzas to arrive. Anna had not seen Michael Hudson and did not know if he was on shift. She hoped he'd come outside if he was.

There were many people out, patrons on the patio and res-idents on the streets. She didn't notice the short man wearing an old motorcycle leather walking along the sidewalk in front of the restaurant, as he was one of many. So she was startled when he reached over the railing and lifted her iPhone off the table where she had placed it. For a moment, as she took in the event, she simply watched him sprint north on Eleventh.

Anna shouted, "Hey!" and Rick registered the situation and came out of his chair. He placed a hand on the railing, leaped over it athletically, and broke into a run almost as soon as his feet hit the sidewalk below. He was in pursuit of the man, who had cut right on Newton and was already out of sight.

Minutes later, inside the dining room, Michael, who was picking up a rack of glassware at the service end of the bar, saw some folks standing by the north windows, talking excitedly and looking out to the street. Michael went there and observed Anna, standing by a table at the edge of the patio, gesturing to Angelos Valis, who had gone outside and was writing something down on a notepad. And then Michael saw Anna's husband, Rick, walking back to the patio from up around Newton Street. He looked angry.

Michael waited for Angelos to come back inside. Angelos grabbed a waiter and said, "That couple out there, the lady that just got robbed? I'm buying their dinner."

The waiter said, "You got it, boss."

"What got stole?" said Michael.

"Her phone," said Angelos. "Dude grabbed it right off their table and booked."

"I know her," said Michael.

"Yeah, they're regulars," said Angelos. "I gotta call the police. Then I'll look at the video. Good thing we got a camera out there."

"Mind if I look too?" said Michael.

"When it slows down here," said Angelos, "come upstairs."

ANNA WAS a little shaken up and wanted a drink, but not at the District Line, so on the walk home they stopped at bar on

Georgia that they both liked. Seated at the stick, both of them nursing beers, Rick watched Anna's lips move, though she was not speaking.

"You're talking to yourself," said Rick.

"I'm pissed off."

"You had your passcode in place, right? Your phone was locked?"

"Always."

"Was the Find My iPhone thing enabled?"

"No." Anna shook her head. "And don't say you told me to do that. I *know* you did."

"Okay. When we get home we'll get on the laptop and change your Apple password. And then we'll call our carrier and disable the account. It's a pain in the ass. But it's no big deal."

"City life," she said.

"This shit happens everywhere," said Rick. "You want to move to the suburbs or something?"

Anna smiled with admiration. "You were out of your chair like a rocket."

"Little fucker got a jump on me. Once he made the right on Newton, he disappeared." Rick squeezed her hand. "Let's settle up and go home."

ANGELOS VALIS had a small office off the upstairs dining room where he kept top-shelf liquor, his files, and a government-style metal desk. On the desk was a fifteen-inch monitor. Security cameras were in place in both dining rooms, and an outdoor camera had been mounted and pointed at the patio and street. Angelos and Michael were watching a replay of the robbery. Also in the office was Joe, the short wannabe boxer and pizza chef, who was interested in anything that involved conflict and drama.

"That's him," said Angelos.

Michael watched as a stocky dude, small as an early teen but a man by age, wearing one of those leather jackets had zippers on the sleeves and chest, grabbed Anna's phone off the table and sped on foot up the street. Anna stood up, pointed at the man, and then her husband leaped over the railing and gave chase. Looked like her man was in shape.

"You guys recognize him?"

"I don't," said Michael, and he looked over at Joe. Joe's eyes registered something but he held his tongue.

"Well, I reported it to the MPD," said Angelos. "That's all I can do."

Angelos took a call on his cell from the bartender and stepped out of the room. When Angelos was well gone, Michael turned to Joe.

"You know that guy, amigo?" said Michael.

"Who?"

"Don't play. The man who boosted the phone."

"Yes, I know him," said Joe. "He wear that jacket all the time. He probably stole that too. Lives with some men I know who work in kitchens, like me. Sometimes we drink beer at their house. He doesn't work. He is a bum."

"So you know where he stay at?"

"*Sí,* Tall Man," said Joe, and his eyes smiled. "What are you gonna do?"

* * *

THE CELL on Ornazian's nightstand was buzzing, but he didn't answer it because he was busy making love to his wife. He gathered Sydney's thick, muscular thighs around his waist. She flexed her inner muscles and tightened herself around him.

"Uh," he said.

Sydney chuckled low. "You like that?"

"*Fuck,* yeah," he said and kissed her full mouth. She made a small grunt of pleasure as he touched bottom.

Their pit mix Blue was asleep on one of two cushions in the room. Their other dog, Sydney's protector, sat beside their bed, watching them fuck. Whitey had been whining for the last ten minutes.

"Stupid animal," said Ornazian.

"He thinks you're hurting me."

"I am."

She was getting there. He could tell by her cooling lips and her escalating moans. He turned her over because that was how she liked to finish. He gripped her shoulders for purchase and she reached between her legs and worked herself.

"Apo piso," said Ornazian.

"Huh?"

"'From behind.' It's Greek."

"I know it's Greek. They invented it. Don't stop."

She burst with a long shudder.

They rested, and then she said, "Now you," because he had controlled it and held himself back. She propped some pillows against the headboard and told him to sit and lean back, and then she pushed his legs apart and got between them. She went to him with vigor.

"Look up at me when you do that," said Ornazian.

"Who made you king?" she said.

"*You* did."

MICHAEL STOOD on Princeton Place in Park View around two thirty a.m., after the bars had officially closed. He was near a group of low-rent row homes, painted brick, no stoops, no porches, on the south side of the street. The man in the leather jacket, whose name was Guillermo and who went by Gil, lived in one of the homes. He was not there now. This Michael knew because Joe had asked a female friend to call the house and see if he was in. The person who picked up the phone told the woman that Gil was out "having beers."

Some of the bars citywide stayed open and served past their closing time, but Michael was patient and energized. He himself had just recently clocked out of work. He was not tired.

Around three a.m., a man in a black jacket with multiple zippers—surely Gil—came up from Georgia Avenue, walking unsteadily. Michael crossed the street and headed toward him. The man would be naturally hesitant at this hour to see a big man approach him on a dark street, but his machismo prevented him from stepping to the side, and as they neared each other Michael grabbed him by the lapels of his jacket, lifted him off his feet, and slammed him onto the hood of a nearby Nissan sedan.

Michael held Gil fast with one hand, bore his full weight down on him, and violently pressed his forearm across his throat.

"You stole a phone tonight," said Michael.

Gil looked into Michael's unyielding eyes. "The phone no work."

"I ain't ask for no review."

"Eh?"

"Give it up."

The swell inside Michael was familiar.

ORNAZIAN AND Sydney lay in bed, naked atop the sheets, his arm under her, her head on his broad chest. Now the room was quiet, as Whitey had joined Blue in sleep. With his free hand, Ornazian traced the curve of her rump.

"You're fine as shit, girl."

"Is that a compliment?"

"You *are*. I showed Thaddeus that photo of you and he was like, *Damn.*"

"You're bad."

"Proud, is all."

"I'm still carrying fifteen extra pounds from the babies. I could stand to lose a few."

"Please don't. You're perfect as you are."

"You just like me."

"I do, indeed."

"I want to look like Diana Ross in 1967."

"I'd leap over a hundred Diana Rosses just to touch your hand."

"You're sweet."

"I mean it." He did too.

Sydney looked up at him. "What are you working on with Thaddeus?"

"Couple of things," said Ornazian. "We're gonna be flush."

"I don't care about that."

"It's for our family. Besides, I got a life insurance policy. Half a mil. Even covers suicide, in case all your talking drives me to it."

"I don't like it when you joke about that," said Sydney. "I worry."

"Don't," he said. "Everything's good."

Sydney left the room to use the toilet in the hall. Ornazian reached over to the nightstand to check his phone.

Michael Hudson had called.

SEVENTEEN

THE NEXT day, Ornazian pulled into a north–south alley off Kansas Avenue and drove to where it joined another alley at a T. There he came upon a freestanding red-brick garage large enough to hold four vehicles. A sign above the bays read FRIENDLY AUTO RE-PAIRS. The establishment was licensed to work on cars.

A man with a full head of tight black curls stepped out of the garage rubbing his hands on a shop rag. His name was Berhanu and his true business was off-the-books rental cars known as hacks. He accepted only cash, which served him and his clients well. There was no paper trail.

Ornazian got out of his Ford amid the frenzied barks of alley dogs. He walked through an open chain-link gate, wide enough to allow the entry and exit of vehicles, and shook Berhanu's hand.

"*Selam,* Berhanu," said Ornazian. "How's your family?"

"Thanks be to God, Phil. They are well. And yours?"

"We're good."

Ornazian and Berhanu were both Eastern Orthodox Christians and when they greeted each other, they observed certain rituals. They were not close friends but their common religion connected them in an unspoken way.

"What do you have for me?"

"Come inside."

They walked into the garage that was lit by drop lamps. A large tool bench ran along the back of the bays. Berhanu's man, a beer alcoholic named Donnie, was seated on an overturned milk crate, drinking Budweiser from a can. He was a good mechanic when sober. Though he recognized Ornazian, he said nothing to him upon his entrance. Instead, Donnie got up and walked out of the garage.

There were three cars in the bays. Two of them were imports: a high-horse Lexus LS460 and an E-Series Benz that Berhanu kept for big rollers. The third was a nineties-era Chevy Impala SS, black over gray, with five-spoke aluminum wheels. Its bumpers, grille, and rocker panels were black and not chromed. The Impala SS had been the shot-across-the-bow for the modern muscle-car sedan. Ornazian went to it immediately. It was a car he had coveted when he was a young man but could not afford. He opened the driver's-side door and inspected the interior. The front buckets were as spacious as La-Z-Boys and the rear bench was as big as a sofa.

"A '94?" said Ornazian.

"How did you know?"

"The trans arm is on the column. Chevy moved the shifter to the floor later on."

"Very good."

"You removed the spoiler."

"It attracts attention," said Berhanu.

"So do the pipes."

"If you want unflavored water but still fast, go with the Lexus. Three hundred and eighty horses."

"You can keep your rice burner. I need space on this one. My driver goes around six four."

"It's a living room inside. Wilt Chamberlain's Afro wouldn't touch the headliner."

"Good shape?"

"Donnie's done a nice job with it. Heavy-duty suspension and brakes. New de Carbon shocks. It's not a screamer off the line but it gets up to sixty very quickly." Berhanu shrugged. "Basically, it's a four-door Vette."

"My jeans are getting tight."

"You and your penis."

"It's a way of life."

"So, we are good?"

Ornazian nodded. "Plates?"

"I'll provide."

Berhanu got his license plates from the long-term parking lots of the three local airports. He also had an extensive network of garage attendants in the area who helped him from time to time. Many attended his church on Illinois Avenue in Northwest.

Ornazian and Berhanu negotiated a price.

"Ciao," said Ornazian to Berhanu before leaving.

"Ciao, Phil."

Ornazian went to his car, where Donnie stood, his smartphone in his hand. As Ornazian approached, Donnie slipped the phone in his coverall pocket and walked away. Ornazian said nothing to Donnie. He didn't trust drunks.

Ornazian's plan for the day was to go out to Glen Echo

157

Heights and surveil the Kelly residence. With luck, Terry Kelly would return home for one of his periodic visits. Ornazian would have dinner with his family and then do a night surveillance on Gustav and his men. This time he would follow the fat man out to his home in Hyattsville in an effort to ascertain a pattern. So far, Gustav had consistently gone from the brothel straight to his home, driven by Cesar in the Range Rover. The thin man took the Mustang, their follow car.

But now, sitting in his Ford in the alley, Ornazian would call Michael Hudson, give him the address of the woman he was looking for, and tell Michael that he had found a car.

AFTER HIS day shift at the restaurant, Michael went to his mother's house, read his latest book out on the porch, and walked Brandy. Then he showered and dressed in a nice shirt and jeans. He brushed out his Timbs till they looked fresh, grabbed his watch cap, and left the house. Shadows had lengthened on the street.

Michael walked up to Warder Place in Park View and went up the steps to a tan-brick row house with bars on the first-floor windows. He stood on a small porch that could only hold one chair and knocked on the front door. Soon the door opened and Anna Byrne stood in the open frame.

"Michael," said Anna. She was obviously taken by surprise but her eyes and body language said that he was fine.

"It's me," said Michael. "I got your phone."

Michael pulled her iPhone from his back pocket and handed it to her across the threshold.

"God," she said. "How did you get this?"

"Listened to the street telegraph. Wasn't all that difficult."

"Thank you. Thank you so much."

"I put it on my mother's charger. So you should be able to use it now."

Anna powered up her phone and entered her password. Multiple messages and texts loaded. She had not yet notified the carrier of the theft, as Rick had told her to do. Rick would have said that she was foolish. She preferred to think of herself as an optimist.

"Thank you," she said again, and then they stood there, him on the porch, she inside her home.

It was obvious to Michael that she was not going to ask him in, and why should she? She had known him only as an offender, not as a free man.

"Your husband home?" he said.

"Not yet," she said. "Hey, you want to go for a walk? Let me buy you a beer or something. It's the least I can do."

"I don't drink," said Michael. "But I'll sit with you."

"Give me five minutes," she said.

"I'll wait for you here," said Michael. He was sparing her the discomfort of asking him to wait outside.

THEY WALKED down to Georgia Avenue. Anna had her hair down and she had changed into jeans and a sweater over a black button-down shirt. Not provocative in any way, but cleaned up. Michael thought she looked nice.

Anna suggested a place called the Midlands, a beer garden

with outdoor seating and open doors that led to an indoor bar area with a pool table. They sat at a picnic table because it was warm enough. Lights were hung on strings on wood beams in an arbor-type atmosphere. Longtime neighborhood residents were mixed with new ones. A smoker had been set up and someone was cooking some kind of meat that smelled good. People brought their dogs here, and water and treats were provided. There were many young men with beards.

Anna sipped a lager and Michael had a ginger ale. She asked him how he'd found her home. It wasn't an accusation. She was curious.

"Dude I know who's in the business of locating people. He helped me out." He meant Phil Ornazian. "I didn't mean to, like, invade your privacy."

"You didn't."

"Since I'm being truthful, I looked at your credit card receipt from that first night I saw you at the DL. Said your husband's name was Byrne. It confused me, 'cause, you know, you go by Anna Kaplan at the jail."

"A lot of women don't take their husband's last names when they get married."

"For real?"

"You're kidding me, right?"

"Yes."

"Well, if you happen to run into anyone we both know, I hope you'll keep my secret."

"Don't worry, I won't give you up."

"I didn't think you would."

Michael relaxed. He was grateful she hadn't asked for details on how he'd retrieved her phone. "What kind of name is Kaplan?"

"I'm Jewish. And my full name is Annalisa. It means 'grace' or 'devoted to God.' My parents are full-on American, but they met on a kibbutz when they were backpacking through Europe after college. They were very into the Israeli-name thing."

"My mother named me Michael. It was 1989, and she was very into that Michael Jordan thing."

Anna smiled and sipped her beer. One of the owners' dogs, a big friendly beast, bounded over to their table and sniffed Michael's outstretched hand. Michael liked this place. He felt comfortable here, though he recognized no one and most of the customers were not the kind of people he'd come up with. He looked through the fence to the right of the Midlands and saw a storefront sign for a place called Wall of Books.

"*Dag,* they got a bookstore here?"

"Yes," said Anna. "They buy and sell used books there."

"Must've opened that while I was away. I can't believe all the changes. This was kinda rough around here, before your time. What with the Park Morton homes right down the street. I used to see all kinds of go-go shows at the Capitol City Ball Room, right there." Michael motioned with his head toward a big boxy building on Georgia.

"People called it the Black Hole, right?" said Anna.

"You know about that?"

"I've heard about it from my neighbors. What do you think of all the changes around here? Is it bad?"

"Not all. What do you call that, when you're looking back, and it seems better than it really was?"

"Nostalgia."

"Right. Sometimes I feel like a stranger in my own neighborhood, but long as too many people don't get pushed out their homes, I guess the changes are good. All these new businesses, bars, and things…the Safeway up the street? Those are jobs that weren't there before."

"But people do get displaced."

"Sure do. That's what that book was about. *The Beautiful Things That Heaven Bears*?"

"You read it?"

"Yeah."

"I chose it for our book club," said Anna. "It might have been a bad call."

"The fellas didn't like it?"

"It's not that. Some of them made the cardinal mistake of reviewing. They chastised the author for not writing the story they *wanted* him to write."

"I bet I know why. They couldn't understand why that Ethiopian dude, Sepha, didn't get with that woman, Judith. I mean, like, get with her all the way. Right?"

Anna chuckled. "Yes. You remember Donnell? He said, 'Why did I take all that time to read that book if that dude wasn't gonna consommé the relationship?' And then he said, 'I want my money back.'"

Michael laughed. "Sounds like that fool."

"The book did generate discussion. Which is, you know, what good books should do."

"I guess the author was saying, you can have a deep friendship with someone without having that physical thing."

"Among other things, yes." She looked him over. "So you're reading a lot."

"Like a mad dog. That's 'cause of you."

"Stop it."

They exchanged phone numbers. Maybe it was the one beer that had altered Anna's judgment. But she trusted him. She took her phone back and almost as an afterthought did a check-in text with her husband: *Got my phone back. I'm out taking a walk. I'll be home soon.* It wasn't exactly a lie.

After Anna had paid the bill, they went to the bookstore that was steps away. They browsed separately in the wooden stacks and Anna took something up to the register. She found Michael in the fiction section. He looked energized. Anna handed him a used paperback. It was a novel called *Northline*.

"That's for you," said Anna. "It's one of my favorites."

Michael was touched and speechless. To cover his emotion, he read the copy on the back.

"Says here it's set in Las Vegas and Reno," said Michael. "I never been out that way."

"I hope you like it," said Anna.

HE WALKED her back to her house at dusk. He suggested they go north on Quebec Street instead of taking Princeton, where he had strong-armed the man who'd stolen her phone the night before. He didn't want to risk being recognized.

"How's it going?" said Anna, looking up at him.

"You mean my life?"

"Yes."

"I like my job. Sayin, it's okay for now, till I figure out what's next." He flashed on Ornazian and what they were planning to do. "It's always a challenge when you come uptown."

"What's that mean, *come uptown?*"

"It's just somethin dudes say, when they come out. *Uptown* doesn't mean it's fancy. But it's way better than where you been, because it's home."

"So…"

"It's a little bit of a struggle, is all. But I reckon I'll be fine."

As they approached the corner of Quebec and Warder, Anna told him she'd walk the rest of the way herself. Michael knew it was because of her husband. She didn't want her man to see them together. He understood.

"Thank you for getting my phone back," she said.

"Ain't no thing," said Michael. "Be easy, Anna."

They went their separate ways. She looked over her shoulder as she neared her house. Michael was adjusting the watch cap on his head, tilting it just so.

WALKING SOUTH on Warder, he saw Carla Thomas sitting on her porch alone, illuminated by candlelight. He went up the steps and joined her. She was drinking a glass of red wine, listening to some Erykah Badu, casting *Mama's Gun* from her phone to a Bluetooth speaker she had set up on the porch.

"Big man," said Carla. "Come up and set."

"Looks like you're at peace," said Michael, taking a seat beside her.

"Not too often I get time to myself."

"Where's Alisha?"

"She's at a friend's house," said Carla. "I got to pick her up in a couple of hours. And my grandmother's out too. She playin bingo at her church."

"So..."

"That's right. I'm alone."

Michael said nothing. Words of seduction failed him. He was out of practice.

Carla stood up and lifted her glass of wine off the table. She gathered up the speaker and her phone as well.

"You comin in?"

"I'd like to."

"Bring that candle with you, Mike."

With gratitude and anticipation, he watched the sway of her hips as she walked through the door. Michael picked up the candle and followed her into the house.

EIGHTEEN

ORNAZIAN SCOOPED up Michael Hudson a few blocks north of his mother's house on Sherman Avenue, at his request. Darkness had fallen hours earlier. Ornazian stopped at the corner, let the vehicle idle, got out of the car, and went around to the passenger bucket. Michael slipped under the wheel, powered back his seat, and let his long frame settle.

"Impala SS," said Michael, failing to keep the pleasure from his voice. "Haven't drove one of these in a long while." He gripped and released the steering wheel and studied the instrument panel.

"Told you I'd hook you up. Let's head out. Our man's in Ward Nine."

Michael recognized the somewhat derogatory term for Prince George's County but made no comment on it, as he had no skin in that game. He pulled down on the transmission arm and went east.

"Where exactly?" said Michael.

"You know Beaver Heights?"

"On the *Mer*'land side of Eastern Ave."

"That's right."

As Michael drove, Ornazian watched him get a feel for the Impala. On Kenilworth Avenue, when the road was clear, Michael punched the gas. Cruising smoothly on the up-market shocks, the sedan picked up speed like an airplane on a runway.

"Take care on the corners," said Ornazian. "It wallows."

"What's that mean?"

"It doesn't hug the road too well."

"It's a straight-line runner," said Michael. "Always was."

"You had one of these?"

"For a day."

They parked in the lot behind the complex of buildings where Thaddeus Ward had his business. Michael put the SS at the end of a row of three black cars while Ornazian used his cell to alert Ward to their arrival. Soon Ward, clad in dark clothing, walked across the lot, chest out. Michael checked out his swagger and his neatly trimmed gray mustache.

"Man's cocky," said Michael. "And old."

"Not too old," said Ornazian. "He can still do it. Pop the lid."

Ward retrieved a couple of duffel bags from the trunk of the Crown Vic and dropped them in the open trunk of the SS. He got into the backseat of the Impala, reached across the console, and shook Michael's hand.

"Thaddeus Ward."

"Michael Hudson."

Michael drove out of the lot.

* * *

THEY PARKED on a side street in Columbia Heights, a couple of blocks west of Georgia, near the bar with the nine ball painted on its light box. Down the block, a kid sat on a chair outside a row house, holding a cell in his hand. The black Range Rover and the blue Mustang were parked nearby.

Michael looked around. "Couple of security cameras on this street. They could be recording our license plates."

"Not to worry," said Ornazian. "The plates on this car don't match the registration."

"Pretty bold," said Michael. "To have this place right here, where folks live."

"It won't be here all that long, most likely," said Ward. "They move these whorehouses around."

"How can they operate without getting busted?" said Michael.

"By the time you get a warrant from a judge, the place is gone. Hard to hit a moving target."

"Someone's gettin paid," said Michael, his eyes in the rearview. He was looking at Ward in the backseat.

Ward spoke with patience. "I worked Vice for a long time, young man. Never knew of any vice cops who were that dirty. Some of the fellas I worked with got a little close to the girls, if you know what I mean. Tipped 'em off in advance if there was a bust about to go down, like that. But that's different. That's just being human." Ward took a stick of gum from his pocket, unwrapped it, and popped it in his mouth. "The chief eliminated the vice squad units in the District in 2015. So there's less manpower to deal with this mess now. Not making excuses. Explaining it to you, is all."

"So you were all clean," said Michael, pushing it.

"I'm only speaking on my experience in the MPD. There's whorehouses in Montgomery County, one I've seen myself.

Right in a residential district, on the edge of that neighborhood where the lefties live. You drive by in the summertime, you see the girls sitting in the window boxes on the second floor. A blind man can see they're trickin. I don't know how the police out there can let that ride. *I* wouldn't. I hate motherfuckers who run women. I just do."

Ornazian let Ward's anger simmer. It was good to have Ward jacked up on his bad memories.

An old car with rusted rear quarter panels pulled up to the row house. The kid spoke into his cell as several men got out of the hooptie and went inside the brothel.

"They're about to get some," said Ward.

"Our man should be coming out soon," said Ornazian, glancing at his watch. It was two a.m.

A half hour later, Gustav, in his ill-fitting sport jacket, and Cesar, his second, came out of the house. Cesar carried two briefcases. There was no third man.

"Where's the dude who drives the follow car?" said Ward.

"I don't know," said Ornazian. "Whether he's with them or not, we have to do this tonight. Tomorrow's Monday. Gustav might start laundering the cash."

Cesar put the briefcases in the backseat and got behind the wheel as Gustav climbed up into the passenger seat. The Range Rover pulled off the curb.

"Cook it," said Ornazian.

Michael turned the ignition. He rested his wrist on the transmission arm. "Waitin on your word."

"Ease up," said Ornazian. "We know where they're going."

* * *

GUSTAV LIVED at the southern edge of Hyattsville, just above the North Brentwood line, in Maryland. He was west of Rhode Island Avenue, down a road that backed to Northwest Branch parkland. At the head of the street, the pavement had buckled into a V, and Michael negotiated it carefully. At Ornazian's direction, Michael killed the Impala's headlamps and rolled slowly alongside Gustav's property.

"Keep going," said Ornazian.

As he followed the curve in the road, which wound around to the front of the house, Michael saw that the street led to a dead end, where short concrete pylons flanked a bike path leading into the park. The pylons were framed by trash cans on the left and the edge of a wooded area on the right. Michael studied the space on the right and gauged its width.

"What's that lead to?"

"The Northwest Branch trail. Runs along the Anacostia River."

"The Anacostia comes all the way out here?"

"We're not far from the District. You good?"

"Yeah."

Michael turned the car around and faced it back out toward the highway. He parked along a post-and-board fence that was in disrepair and let the engine run.

Gustav's residence was a two-story affair with white plank siding situated on a half an acre of weedy land. Lights were on inside the house. The back of the house held a deck and it gave on to more land running to woods that bordered a soccer field. The Range Rover was parked in the gravel driveway. There were no streetlights. There was only one other house on the street and it was relatively distant and up on a rise.

Ornazian reached up and disabled the dome light. He turned toward Michael. "I'm gonna give you a two-way."

"Okay."

"If you need to contact us, use the radio, not your phone. Call me Number One if you want to address me. Don't use my name."

"Go it."

"Pop that lid."

Ornazian and Ward got out of the car and went to the open trunk. Ward bent in low and, with a mini Maglite in his mouth, unzipped the duffel bags. They slipped nitrile gloves onto their hands, and then they tooled up, Ward with his Remington shotgun and Glock 17, Ornazian with the .38. Ward stuffed various sizes of plastic cuffs and a Buck knife into his jacket pocket while Ornazian grabbed a set of two-way Motorola radios. Last, they fitted stockings over their faces. Ward closed the trunk's lid.

Ornazian went to the open driver's-side window of the Impala and handed Michael a radio. He spoke softly. "Use channel eleven."

Ornazian nodded at Ward over the roof. They went to the fence and walked into the yard through a space where a board had fallen, then over to the rear deck. Ornazian got down and crawled under it, through gas cans, empty beer cans, and brown leaves, and came out on the other side. Now Ward and Ornazian flanked the deck, both in a crouch.

Ward looked into the double glass doors at the rear of the house. The bodyguard, Cesar, was holding a tumbler of something amber over ice, absently watching a soccer game on a wide-screen TV. His back was to the doors. Gustav was not in sight.

Ward stood up to his full height and moved around the corner of the deck, deliberately triggering the exterior security lamp mounted on the second floor of the house. Light flooded the yard and Ward immediately crouched back down. They waited and listened and soon heard the unlocking of the back doors. Then the sound of heavy footsteps on the deck. Then the rack of a slide.

Ward stood, pumped a round into the Remington, and pointed its muzzle at Cesar. Cesar held a semiautomatic in his right hand.

Ornazian came into the light, snicked back the hammer of the revolver, and trained it on Cesar. Cesar heard the trigger lock back but he did not look at Ornazian or react.

"Drop it," said Ward.

Cesar, expressionless, raised his gun and trained it on Ward. Ward made a step forward but otherwise did not flinch.

"How about I murder you?" said Cesar.

"How 'bout we murder each other?" said Ward.

The three of them stood in the harsh yellow light of the floodlamp. Time passed.

"Why have you come?" said Cesar.

"We're here to rob your boss," said Ward.

Cesar considered this.

"Is not my money," Cesar said. He lowered his gun and placed it on the deck.

AS THEY went into the house, they heard Gustav calling out for Cesar. Cesar looked back at the armed men behind him.

Ornazian put his finger to his lips and Ward made a motion with his chin. They were telling Cesar not to speak and to keep moving forward.

He led them past a kitchen, where there were chairs set around an oval table. Then the three of them went down a hall to an open bedroom door. They entered the room all at once and Gustav rose from the bed, startled. The briefcases were atop the bed.

Gustav looked angrily at Cesar, who maintained his unemotional expression.

"What is this?" said Gustav.

"I ain't tell you to speak," said Ward.

Gustav cursed creatively in Spanish. Something about shitting in their mothers' milk.

Ward, who understood a good deal of Spanish, thought it was a curious comment but let it pass. He glanced at Ornazian. "Go to the kitchen and bring back a couple of those chairs."

Ornazian left the room. Ward held the shotgun on Cesar, which was an insult to Gustav, telling him he was not a threat. With his left hand Ward pulled back his jacket to show them the grip of his Glock.

Ornazian returned with the chairs and set them at the foot of the bed. They were ladder-back in design, constructed of metal and tubular steel.

"Sit down," said Ward to Cesar.

Cesar sat. As Ornazian covered them with his revolver, Ward used large plastic cuffs to bind Cesar's feet and smaller ties to secure his hands behind the chair. Cesar did not resist.

When he was done, Ward said to Gustav, "Strip."

"Eh?"

"Take your clothes off, fat man. Everything."

Gustav reddened but took off his clothing piece by piece, folding each item neatly and placing it on the shag-carpeted floor. He stood naked before them. He was misshapen, with saddlebag boobs and a stomach that fell in waves over his groin.

"Damn," said Ward. "You are one fucked-up-lookin individual. Where'd you get them girl-titties at? I mean, you *look* like a man with your clothes on, but *shit*..."

Ward continued along those lines, breaking Gustav down, commenting on his uncut penis, its lack of size, and his generally revolting appearance. Then he tied him to the second chair the same way he had bound Cesar. Ornazian hadn't uttered a word. The psych game was Ward's specialty and he was doing fine.

After Gustav had been secured, Ornazian opened the briefcases and inspected their contents. Both were filled with rubber-banded cash, but the amount seemed unremarkable. Twenties, mostly, with a smattering of fives and tens. Ornazian shut the lids.

"Where's the rest of it?" said Ward.

"Huh?" said Gustav.

"High-rollin pimp like you, I know you have a stash."

Gustav stared straight ahead.

"Never mind," said Ward. "We'll find it our *own* selves."

Ornazian and Ward tossed the bedroom sloppily. They checked every drawer. Ward used his Buck knife to slash open the mattress and box spring, then swept everything off the dresser top because it felt good. Finally, Ornazian checked the closet. Behind the hung-up clothing was a safe set in the wall.

It was the type found in a hotel. There were decaled instructions on its face.

"Well," said Ward.

Gustav hocked on the carpet.

"It's your shag," said Ward. "Spit on it, you got a mind to."

"Give us the combination," said Ornazian.

When Gustav said nothing, Ward said to Ornazian, "Try the usual."

Ornazian began entering the most common four-digit combinations into the pad of the safe. Starting with 1-1-1-1, moving on to 2-2-2-2, and so forth. When he got past 9-9-9-9, with no result, he went with the tried-and-true 1-2-3-4.

"Nothing," said Ornazian. Beneath his stocking mask, his face was damp with sweat. All of them were perspiring profusely now. The room stank of it.

"What's your birthday, Goo-stav?" said Ward.

Gustav did not reply.

Ward went to the clothing pile, kicked it apart, and picked up Gustav's pants. He lifted his wallet out of the back pocket and opened it. He extracted the cash in the wallet and stuffed the bills in his own pocket. Then he slipped Gustav's driver's license out and read it.

"December seventeenth, 1974," said Ward. "Try seventeen seventy-four."

Ornazian punched the numbers into the grid but the safe did not open.

"Nope," he said.

"Okay, try twelve seventy-four. One-two-seven-four."

Ornazian entered this combination and a green light glowed on the face of the safe. Its door sprang open.

Gustav muttered something unintelligible as Ornazian reached into the safe and extracted several banded stacks of hundred-dollar bills. He made a couple of trips to the bed to fit the new-found cash in with the old. He snapped the briefcases shut.

"Chinga tu hermana," said Gustav, tears of anger in his eyes.

"Why'd you have to say that?" said Ward. He reversed his grip on the shotgun and with great force pushed its butt into Gustav's chest. The chair tipped back and Gustav crashed to the floor. His hands, bound behind him, were crushed by his own weight. Gustav cried out.

Cesar looked up at Ward. *"Nos encontraremos otra vez."*

"Maybe," said Ward. "But not tonight."

They left the house the way they'd come. The security light activated as they stepped out onto the deck. Ward kicked Cesar's gun over the edge before he took the steps down to the yard. Then they crossed the yard and passed through the space in the fence. Michael popped the trunk's lid as he saw them approach the car. They dumped their weapons, gear, and the briefcases into the trunk, then their stocking masks and gloves. They closed the trunk and got into the Impala, Ornazian in the front bucket, Ward on the back bench.

"Let's go," said Ornazian.

Just as he spoke, a car turned right off of Rhode Island Avenue and stopped at the head of the street, before the buckle in the road. The driver hit his high beams, blowing his head-lights fully into their eyes.

"It's a Mustang," said Michael. He drew his seat belt across his lap and seated it in the latch.

"The follow car," said Ward.

"He's not moving," said Michael.

"Go," said Ornazian.

Michael put the transmission arm in reverse, placed his hand on the top of Ornazian's bucket, and turned his head to look behind him. He hit the gas. The Impala slid into the curve but Michael corrected and headed for the concrete pylons. As he did, Ornazian saw the Mustang accelerate and hit the V in the buckled road. The beams of the Ford's headlights went down and then up into the sky as the car dropped into the V and shot back out of it.

"Watch those barriers," said Ward, but Michael had swerved to the left of them, crossing the narrow area of brush that bordered the woods. He drove in reverse down the path along the soccer field, and when he came to the T of it, he swung the wheel, braked, and slammed the shifter down into drive. Headlights off, he headed down the wide asphalt path. He climbed a steep hill, accelerating rapidly. They could not see over the hill's crest.

"Hey," said Ward. "Slow down."

In his rearview, Michael could see the Mustang in pursuit. He did not slow down. At the top of the hill the Impala caught air as all four wheels left the earth, and for a moment they were staring down the other side of the hill as they descended, and when they hit the pavement, a steep ravine to their left, they were jostled wildly and nearly slid off the edge, but Michael, two hands on the wheel, steadied the car. At the bottom of the hill the land leveled and Michael pinned the pedal, negotiating the slight curves artfully. He looked again into his rearview mirror. The Mustang had gone over the crest of the hill, hit air, and come down sloppily. It slid over the edge of the ravine and came to a stop by the rocky bulkhead at the water's edge.

"He's done," said Michael.

Michael eased off the gas pedal. They rolled on the path beside the river, the moonlight shimmering bright on its water. Soon they came to a road and a parking lot. There were more pylons ahead and Michael jumped off the path and into the lot, then took the road. He turned on his headlights.

"The next traffic light is Hamilton," said Ornazian. "Take a left onto that and then continue on to Queens Chapel Road. It becomes Michigan Avenue."

"I know where we're at," said Michael.

From the backseat, Ward began to laugh. Ornazian turned around and smiled. They dapped fists.

"What did Cesar say to you before we left?" said Ornazian.

"He said we'd meet again."

The men grew quiet. As they crossed over into the District, Thaddeus Ward closed his eyes and drifted off to sleep.

NINETEEN

HE HAD clocked out, and the weather had broken to warm, so Michael decided to sit outside the restaurant at one of those picnic tables on the patio and read his book before he walked home. He had started in on *Northline*, the novel Anna had bought for him at the store on Georgia Ave. There were a few customers out here, young folks, mostly, who had come by for happy hour, and though they were not particularly boisterous, he found a table away from them where he could read in peace.

At first, Michael hadn't thought this book was to his liking. In the very first chapter, a drunk girl named Allison Johnson has unloving sex with a drug addict named Jimmy Bodie in the bathroom stall of a casino out in Las Vegas. She passes out while they're making it, falls down, and cuts her head. *All right*, thought Michael, *that's just the start of the book. That's to show that the girl has hit bottom and has learned something. Now things are gonna get brighter.* But the girl doesn't learn.

This Bodie dude, a speed freak and all-around loser, comes by her mother's house a couple of days later and begs Allison to forgive him for doing her dirty. And instead of throwing him out, she gives him another chance. They go out to the desert to one of those new-Nazi parties and get all fucked up again on drugs and alcohol, and then she sees Bodie running his hands up inside the skirt of another girl. Michael thinking, *If Allison Johnson is just going to keep being a drunk and keep being a punching bag for this dude, I don't know if I want to keep reading.* He was beginning to wonder why Anna liked the book so much.

But then, in a chapter called "T. J. Watson," an old trucker by that name picks Allison up by the side of the road and drives her back toward Vegas in his rig. She breaks down and cries, confessing that she's pregnant with Bodie's child. T. J. Watson comforts her. Talks to her about choices, and the accidental death of his son, and the love he still shares with his wife after so many years. He tells her about the value of moving forward in life and the moments of beauty that are there if a person can only see them. For Michael, at that point, the book changed. He knew that, in the story, things were going to get much darker for Allison before they got better. But there would be moments of humanity too.

"Mind if join you, young fella?"

Michael looked up. Gerard, the middle-aged mailman, was by his table, standing straight and fit. He was still in his uniform.

"Have a seat."

Gerard signaled a waiter and ordered a draft beer, then sat across from Michael on the bench.

"I've seen you twice here now," said Gerard. "This where you hang out?"

"I work here. I'm down in the kitchen."

"How's that going?"

"Good. I like to work, just like you."

A car with D.C. plates but flying the Dallas Cowboy flags went past them on Eleventh. The blue star was decaled on its rear window.

"I hate to see that," said Michael.

"I do too. But to understand it, you gotta know your history."

"I know the Redskins were the last team to integrate in the NFL, if that's what you mean. My mother told me that. Until they put Bobby Mitchell on the squad. Right?"

Gerard nodded. "That was the early sixties. There's more to it, though. The owner, George Preston Marshall, had always re-sisted the integration of the Redskins. He said it was because his fans in the South wouldn't accept it. See, the Skins were the southernmost team in the NFL at the time, and Marshall owned the radio stations down there where the games were broadcast. He claimed it was an economic thing. But Marshall was straight-up racist too. He just didn't want any black football players on his team. You know the Redskins fight song, where everyone sings that line 'Fight for old D.C.'? It used to be 'Fight for old *Dixie*.' That's how blatant that bullshit was. Black folks picketed, and a sportswriter at the *Post*, Shirley Povich, wrote a rack of ar-ticles against the segregation on the team. When other squads who had black athletes on their rosters played Washington, they wanted to shove it up our asses. So there were a lot of angry folks, but Marshall stood his ground. Then, when he went to get the long-term lease for the new D.C. stadium, he met his Water-loo. President Kennedy sent his interior secretary, Udall was his name, over to speak to Marshall and tell him what time it was. No integration, no thirty-year lease on your stadium."

"They forced the man's hand."

"Yeah, Marshall swallowed the bitter pill, but that didn't change what was in his heart. When he died, his will set up a big charitable foundation to benefit kids in the D.C. area. A clause in that will said that no money would ever go to 'any purpose which supports the principle of racial integration in any form.' His dollars would go only to Caucasian kids. The man was like that, even past his deathbed. Some black Washingtonians who lived through that era would never support the Skins because of Marshall. That's why they're Cowboys fans. And now their kids, grandkids, and great-grandkids follow the star, even though they live in the DMV."

"I still hate to see it," said Michael.

Gerard laughed. "I do too. I root for two teams—the Washington Redskins and anyone who's playing the Dallas Cowboys."

Michael and Gerard touched fists.

"How long you been a mailman?" said Michael.

"Thirty-five years."

"You go to school to get that job?"

"Marion Barry gave me this job."

"That crackhead?"

"Don't say that," said Gerard, suddenly serious. "Let me tell you something about Marion Barry."

The waiter served Gerard his beer. Gerard thanked him, waited for him to drift off.

"I come up in public housing in Southeast. The Eights. This was in the sixties and early seventies. Before the drug epidemic, gangs, street murder, all that mess. Lot of families stayed there, and mine was solid. My father was a good man but he had trouble finding steady work. Around that time, Marion

Barry and a partner, Mary Treadwell, started this company, Pride Incorporated. It was set up to put black men to work, doing stuff like pushing brooms, picking up garbage…basically, cleaning the city up. Doesn't sound too good, but it was work for men who were chronically unemployed. Why they gave it that name. It gave men back their pride.

"My father worked for Pride Incorporated and I saw what it did for him. It made him stand straight. As a kid, I saw by example that this is what a man does. He goes to work every day and he takes care of his family. I knew that, soon as I could, I would go to work too. So when I turned sixteen, my father and mother told me about this new thing, the summer jobs program. It was started by Marion Barry, who by then had become the mayor. The program put kids in the city to work. I went down and signed up for it. Soon I was working in a diner down at Nineteenth and Jefferson for a Greek man named Pete. Because of that program, I got into the culture of work. Around that time, Mayor Barry came to my high school, Ballou, and spoke to us kids. He shook my hand and he looked me in the eye and said, 'Keep on it, son. You're gonna do fine.' He was real. Not like some of these cold-ass mayors we been had since. You never did see them talking to any kids.

"Anyway. After I come out of high school, I wanted a government job, so I went out to Riverdale, in Maryland, and took the postal-service exam. I had a good memory, and on that test they ask you to recall the original order of scrambled numbers. A week later, I got the results in the mail. I had scored highly. I was in."

"Marion Barry take that test for you too?" said Michael.

"Don't be funny." Gerard leaned forward. "Let me tell you

something else. When my mother got diabetes, we put her in a nice, clean retirement care center, one of many that Barry had built east of the Anacostia River when he was mayor. Wasn't any of those places around for folks in those quadrants before he came along.

"And me? I own a house in Hillcrest Heights. Been married to the same woman for thirty-one years. I have a son and a daughter, both college graduates and doing fine on their own. Was I upset when Marion Barry was druggin and doing all that stuff with women? I can tell you that I was very disappointed. But I always supported him. Marion Barry made it possible for a black middle class to rise up in this city. I know he changed *my* life. For real."

"Okay," said Michael. "I hear you."

"Know your history, young man," said Gerard. "It's important. 'Specially now, with all these new folks moving into the city. They don't know shit."

"Let me ask you something," said Michael. "Could I take that postal test?"

"You got a high-school degree?"

"Yes."

"What about your priors? I notice all kinds of things on my route, and I know you been away."

"I'm not carrying any adult convictions," said Michael. "Only some juvenile stuff."

"If it's juvenile, you might be all right. They gonna make you pee in a bottle, though."

"I don't smoke weed. I don't even drink."

"You good with numbers?"

"I am."

"You should think about it, then. U.S. Postal Service been good to me." Gerard stood up and showed Michael his flat stomach. "I walk ten miles a day. They pay me to work out."

Michael smiled. "Let me buy you another beer."

Gerard sat back down. "Don't let me stop you."

They talked until the light began to fade, and then Gerard went on his way.

MICHAEL WALKED home, book in hand. He went by Carla's grandmother's house and was relieved to see that Carla was not home. He had enjoyed her company, and he thought she had enjoyed him too, but he wasn't ready for things to get deep. Not while he was unsettled, as he was now. And anyway, she wasn't the one.

He went into the house and walked on the plastic carpet runners to the kitchen. His mother was cooking dinner.

"Supper gonna be ready soon," said Doretha, looking toward him as she stirred a pot. She had put an Anthony Hamilton CD in her compact stereo, and she was listening to that beautiful song "Hard to Breathe." Sounded like they were in church.

He cut his eyes away from her and said, "I'm gonna go read some."

"I'll call you when it's ready," she said.

Brandy got up from her little bed and followed him to the steps. He started up the stairs and heard Brandy whine. She wanted to go with him but could no longer climb to the second floor. He went back down, gathered Brandy in his arms, and carried her up to his bedroom. He sat on the bed. The dog settled at his feet.

Michael looked across the room at the trophies on his brother's dresser. Thomas, who always did right and had made his place in the world as a productive man. And there was his sister, about to graduate college, already looking ahead at a career in public relations.

Michael glanced at his own dresser. In its top drawer, beneath his underwear, was an envelope containing two thousand dollars in cash. Phil Ornazian had doubled his pay.

Michael hadn't spent a dime of it. He didn't care to look at it or touch it. If he had someone to talk to, he'd say that it was blood money. But he'd taken it. He sure hadn't turned it down. And he suspected that Ornazian would be throwing a shadow on his doorstep again.

He needed to talk to a friend. Anna immediately came to mind. As he thought of her, something moved inside him.

Michael propped a pillow under his head. He opened his book, *Northline*, and began to read. He was deeper into the novel now.

In the book, Allison Johnson has given up her baby for adoption and moved to Reno, Nevada, where she works as a waitress on the graveyard shift in a casino restaurant. She also works part-time in telephone sales with an obese, upbeat woman named Penny. Allison is still drinking heavily and distraught about her child. One night, drunk, she is taken to a house by two men in suits, has sex with both of them, and asks one of the men to beat her. She contemplates suicide. The father of her child, Jimmy Bodie, is threatening to come find her. Her life has come apart. And yet...a scarred, sweet-natured young man named Dan Mahony often sits at her station at the restaurant and makes small talk. He buys her a snow globe on a trip he makes to San Francisco. He treats her to coffee and tries to chat her up. She lies to him about her family and her past. She tells him she doesn't want a boyfriend and he takes it in stride. Clearly, he's smitten. But Allison is not ready to enter into a relationship again, because she's not yet right with herself. Binge-drinking in a bar, she passes out and hits her head. When she comes to, she is carried home by a kindly bartender and his wife.

As Michael read the book, he felt the pain and struggles of Allison Johnson. He was in her pathetic motel room, listening to her Patti Page and Brenda Lee records, hearing her imaginary conversations with that old-time actor Paul Newman. He could see Reno, a smaller, quieter version of Vegas, with its low-rent casinos, chicken-fried-steak specials, laundromats, wood-paneled bars, end-of-the-road hopefuls, and neon signs that bled colors out to the street.

He closed his eyes and imagined it. The book had taken him somewhere else. He was outside himself and his troubled mind.

TWENTY

THE LUNCH crowd at Matisse had faded, leaving Phil Ornazian and Monique as the sole patrons seated at the bar. Monique was on her break from the makeup department and still had another half a day of work. She was wearing her all-black uniform, slacks and a button-down shirt. Black deemphasized her voluptuous figure but could not defeat it.

Ornazian passed an envelope under the bar. Monique took it, glanced inside, and slid the envelope into her handbag. He had given her extra. She had hipped him to Marisol, which had driven him to the robbery of Gustav, ending in what was apparently a very lucrative payday. Her lead had been good.

"You took care of me," said Monique.

"It was a solid tip. You earned it."

"Was it hard?"

"Like cutting butter."

"That easy, huh?" Monique sipped her white wine and placed the glass back on the bar.

"What about you?" said Ornazian. "Everything all right?"

"All good. Something happened recently. I met this married

dude up at the makeup counter. He was shopping with his wife. I could tell she didn't have any kind of fashion sense. Maybe she didn't care about stuff like that, I don't know. But when she drifted off and he got me alone, he told me how sharp I looked. Asked me if I ever did anything on the side to make money. I thought he was tryin to date me, so I told him I was a dancer and that I could do it private, just to dip my toe in the water and see if he was interested. But he said, 'No, it's nothing like that. I was wondering if I could hire you to be a personal shopper for my wife for, like, one afternoon. Suggest some things that would look nice on her, 'cause we're about to go out on an anniversary date.' It was sweet. I did it and I made a couple hundred dollars. I was thinking maybe I could start some kind of business doing that. I do know clothes and shoes."

"Obviously. You always look great."

"Thank you, baby. It's not like I'm gonna quit dating. Can't afford to. Who knows, maybe I'll meet Richard Gere or some shit and he'll take me away."

"How do you know when to get off the bus?" said Ornazian. He was genuinely curious. "I'm asking, how's it end for someone like you?"

"I don't know," said Monique. She got up, drained her wineglass, and gathered her cell and handbag. "How you think it's gonna end for you?"

She kissed his cheek and left the bar.

AT SIX o'clock in the evening, Ornazian met Marisol and her baby daughter in the main hall of Union Station. Marisol was wearing her raincoat over a dress and had one large old suitcase and a jumbo canvas handbag. She was sitting on a bench with her daughter in her lap amid the bustle of rush hour in the station.

"What's her name?" said Ornazian after he greeted Marisol.

The baby looked to be around ten, eleven months old and was wearing a lovely white dress. She had one of those things in her hair, a kind of band with a pink bow, something parents put on their children to announce their gender to the world. Ornazian didn't know what it was called, but no one would mistake this baby for anything but a girl.

"Stephany," said Marisol.

Ornazian took a seat beside them. "She's beautiful."

"She's a good girl."

"Did everything go okay? No problems?"

"Gustav is very angry," said Marisol. "Cesar, he ask all the girls questions."

"And?"

"I did fine. But I am scheduled to work tonight and when I don't come they will be suspicious."

"You'll be long gone. Marisol, you can never come back."

"Why would I?" she said.

Ornazian reached inside his tan Kühl jacket and produced an envelope. He handed it to Marisol.

"Your tickets are in there too. Train and bus."

She looked inside the envelope and blushed. "This is much more than you said."

"I made a lot of money because of you."

"You didn't have to do this."

"Come on. Let's go to your gate."

He wheeled her suitcase and bag and she carried the baby. At the gate for the Crescent Amtrak train, a line had already formed. They stood by a shoeshine stand, at the entrance.

"You're going to take this train to New Orleans. It's about a twenty-five-hour trip. You get in at seven thirty in the morning and then you'll walk about five minutes to where they have the Megabus. Take that to Houston. It's another six hours by bus. I wrote all of this down on a piece of paper so you have it. It's in the envelope too."

"Thank you, Phil."

"Go. Get in line so you two can get a good seat."

He watched to make sure she and her baby were set. Then he walked out of Union Station, his head up. It had been a while since he'd felt this right.

THADDEUS WARD'S residence was on a quiet, three-syllable street in Brightwood, in the Fourth District, where he'd served most of his tenure as a D.C. cop. His house was a detached Colonial, clean and neat, with an alley garage that he used as a workshop. He and his wife, Ida, had raised their daughter, Sharon, here. Sharon had been out on her own since the mid-nineties, and Ida had passed long ago. He'd lived alone for the past ten years.

Sharon had come over without her kids, who were now in high school. Her husband, Virgil Cotton, who owned a couple of fast-food franchises, was at their home in Bowie, keeping an eye on the children and seeing that they completed their homework and chores. Sharon and Virgil were strict Christians. As far as the God thing went, Thaddeus was unconvinced.

They had eaten takeout pizza from the Ledo's over on Georgia, and now they were in what Ward called "the TV room," watching the Wizards flame the Lakers.

"Damn, he's fast," said Ward as they watched John Wall accelerate past two defenders in the lane, corkscrew, and finish.

"We got a lot of pieces," said Sharon, who knew the game. She had played basketball for Coolidge in her day. "Bradley Beal, Otto Porter…"

"Georgetown product," said Ward.

"Markieff Morris was a nice addition."

"Don't forget the Polish Hammer," said Ward. "And the coach. Scott Brooks put it all together, Sharon. We're about to win the division. First time since the seventies. LeBron is still a beast, but the Cavaliers are weak, with their injuries and whatnot. This could be the year for my Bullets."

"They're called the Wizards now, Daddy."

"Not in my house."

She looked at him with fond tolerance. "I better get out of here. Let me just clean this mess up."

Sharon made a couple of trips back and forth to the kitchen as she gathered up the pizza box, soda cans, and plates. Ward would have offered to help her but he knew she'd say no. That's why she came over to the house twice a week, to take care of him. She did the dishes that were in the sink, folded his laundry, and changed the sheets on his bed, whether they needed changing or not. She was way overqualified for housework—hell, she was a copyright attorney for the U.S. government—

but she wanted to do it. It wasn't that she enjoyed cleaning up his place. It eased her conscience.

"Sit down, baby girl," said Ward as Sharon came back into the room.

She sat next to him on the couch. "What?"

"I put some money into the kids' college fund today. A good bit of money, in fact."

"Daddy…"

"I wanted to. There's nothing more important than a good education. I know you and Virgil are successful. You got money, I know. But this will help y'all breathe a little easier. That's all it is. Just want to help you out."

"But you're going to retire. You don't want to think about it but that day will come. I don't want you to come up short."

"I got my pension from the MPD, and the army, *and* I got my Social Security checks. This house *been* paid for. I'm flush. This is extra, Sharon. Investments I made a long time ago that have grown. It's money I don't need. I want it to go to my grandchildren, to give them a leg up. Don't argue with me, now."

"Okay."

"Come here."

They hugged and he walked her to the front door. She was his height. Sharon had got her size from her mother. Ida had been tall and straight of back, a standout athlete in the Inter-High. It had been hard on Ida, so healthy all her life, to have her body deteriorate as rapidly as it did. She was gone two months after her initial diagnosis.

Ward watched Sharon get into her Japanese sedan and drive away.

He didn't need the money, it was true. He was happy to give

his grandchildren the opportunity for college that he himself had not taken. It was a bonus from the jobs, but not the reason he took them. Ward didn't lie to himself and say that what he did with Phil Ornazian was for the kids.

He had met Ornazian a few years back, through another middle-aged veteran of the MPD, an Irishman named Liam Shannon, also out of 4D. Ornazian had a client whose wife had been kidnapped over a drug beef, a street snatch unreported to the police. When there was potential violence involved, Ornazian used ex-cops for his security detail, and Shannon was his point man. Shannon, in effect, rounded up the crew. The first time they worked together, Ornazian saw something in Ward. Ornazian said it was how he handled himself. With authority, he said. He might have added that Ward was aggressive and unafraid.

Shannon was straight and Ward was open to suggestion, so Ornazian began to cut him in on side jobs that relieved criminals of their ill-gotten gains. It had been a good partnership so far. Ward realized that Ornazian was playing on his distaste for men who ran women. Ornazian knew, from an early conversation they'd had, that Ward's sister had been lost to the streets.

Ward had come from a solid blue-collar family. His father worked in a diner and his mother was a line cook in a government-agency cafeteria. They were good people and good role models, but, as many parents discover, that wasn't enough to overcome the influence of their children's peers, or stop their daughter from temporarily losing her teenage mind. Ward's sister, Ella, who had been a church girl and good student, started slipping away at age fifteen and somehow got herself introduced to a man who called himself Ace. Ace was a pimp and an addict who seduced Ella and got her hooked on heroin. She was tricking on the Fourteenth Street corridor by the time she was sixteen. Ace got turned out by another pimp, and from the moment that Ace had been punked, he lost his power and could no longer mack. He was just a heroin addict, no longer a stud. Ella stayed with him because she liked him, but she never slept with him again. They lived together only as junkies. Ella's body was found, stiff as plywood, in a needle pad not long after her eighteenth birthday.

Ward never forgot. But his side work with Ornazian wasn't just about hate, and it wasn't about money. He had been a fierce combat soldier in Vietnam and a driven police officer in D.C. Now he was staring at seventy and the other side of the hill. He knew what was coming, and it was very difficult for him to face it. So he'd hold on to his image of himself for as long as he could. He liked the action. That's really all it was, when you got down to it. He wasn't ready to let that part of himself go.

Not yet.

AS NIGHT settled in, Phil Ornazian parked his car on Wagner Lane in Glen Echo Heights, a community of quiet affluence off MacArthur Boulevard, near the C & O Canal and the Potomac River. He was watching the Kelly residence, a simple brick-and-shingle Cape Cod near the top of the street that had been built when the neighborhood was affordable to the middle class. It was his third trip out here and so far he had come up empty. No Terry Kelly, no Dodge Charger. Just a vanilla Honda Pilot in the driveway that, in the hours of his surveillance, had not moved.

He was in a tough spot. He intended to rob Terry and his friends of the Tiffany bracelet, so he couldn't just go up to the door and question Terry's parents. The usual search programs on his laptop had placed Terry at his childhood home on Wagner and gave no alternative addresses. If Terry didn't show he would have to think of something else. But right now, as he pondered it, there didn't seem to be a something else.

His head began to hurt from all the thinking. Also, he was hungry. He hit the ignition button on the dash and headed back to D.C.

Ornazian met Sydney and the boys at a soul food spot on Second and Upshur, not far from their house. He had money in his pocket and he felt like treating them. His sons loved the fried chicken there and Syd was into their crab cakes. The new owner had spiffed up the place but it still had its charms, which included a nice middle-aged waitress and a wall jukebox featuring seventies R & B. The waitress was obviously a Teddy fan, as she had programmed the juke for a nightlong Harold Melvin and the Blue Notes mix. Sydney, like many Brits, was into the American soul and funk of that glorious decade, and because Ornazian was a native Washingtonian, it was in his blood too. The family had a nice night out. Thankfully, the boys were relatively well behaved.

Out on Upshur they walked to Ornazian's Ford. The father, mother, and sons were all different skin shades, but in Petworth and in Park View, few gave them a second look. This acceptance was one reason that Ornazian was determined not to leave the city. They were in the realm of the norm here. He had once taken the family to a friend's wedding in Vermont and he, his wife, and children had received blatant stares while walking down the street. So much for the progressive North.

Back at the house he rewarded the boys for their good behavior and let them sleep in his and Sydney's bed. Whitey and Blue were snoring, passed out on their cushions nearby. The boys soon drifted off too. Ornazian had Gregg on one side of him, Vic on the other. Gregg was close against him and his scalp warmed Ornazian's chest. Ornazian smiled, thinking, *My puppies.*

Sydney, on the far side of the bed, spoke quietly. "Thanks for dinner, love. We should go out more often together. The boys aren't as wild as they used to be."

"Yes, they are. They just had an off night."

"I'm saying, we'll have more time to do things as a family now. You've finished with this last thing, right?"

"I've got other pots boiling on the stove."

"Then take them off the stove."

"All I'm hearing from you right now is cacophony."

"Huh?"

"From the Greek. *Caco* means 'bad.' *Phony* is 'sound.'"

"Oh my God. That again."

"You're making bad sounds."

"Don't get turned around by money," said Sydney. "That's all I'm saying. What's important is right here, in this bed."

"No need to stress on it, Syd. I've got it wired up tight."

"I can't help it."

"Go to sleep."

The wind picked up and rattled the branches of the oak outside their window. Its shadows crawled across their bed.

TWENTY-ONE

A SECURITY guard had remotely opened the cell doors on the Gen Pop unit from inside the fishbowl, and inmates clad in orange jumpsuits had formed a line leading to a desk that was bolted to the floor. Anna sat behind the desk, her rolling cart of books beside her. She was talking to the man with heavy-lidded eyes and a gravelly voice whose name she could not recall.

"You got *The Adventurers?*" he said.

"It's checked out. How about *The Carpetbaggers?*"

"I guess I could read it again. Jonas Cord is my man."

Anna found a battered paperback of the Harold Robbins favorite and checked it out to the inmate.

Donnell, the sleepy-eyed misdemeanant who had nearly served out his term, stepped up to her and placed *The Passenger* on the table. Donnell had asked Anna for books to help him "figure out" women, and Anna had chosen this one for its female voice and perspective. Also, it was a compelling story, well told.

"I got into this one, Anna. That lady can write the *shit* out of a book."

"Glad you liked it."

"When that girl Tanya broke into those vacation houses and just kinda lived there in the off-season, while the owners weren't around? That was crafty. I can see why this book would be popular. 'Cause, you know, the idea that you can dye your hair a new color, cash in your bank account, change your ID cards, and disappear into thin air? It's kind of everyone's fantasy, right? To have a new start."

"It is for some," she said.

"So what you got for me now?"

Anna took a book off the cart. It was one of Wallace Stroby's crime novels about a professional thief named Crissa Stone. "Try this one. It's got a female protagonist. Written by a man but he gets women right."

Donnell opened the book and read some of the flap copy. "Thank you. I'll let you know what I think."

She logged in the information of his returned book and gave Donnell a DCPL receipt.

Larry, the man up on felony manslaughter charges who had recently found Jesus, was next in line.

"Miss Anna."

"Larry. Here you go."

She handed him a slim copy of *The Red Pony*. Since the book club had read *Of Mice and Men*, Larry had asked for more "Mr. Steinbeck." She had erred in giving him *East of Eden*, which he returned unfinished, saying it was "too slow and too long." She thought this one would work better for him.

Larry inspected the cover art, a lovely black-and-white photograph of a grazing horse, circa 1926, taken by Albert Renger-Patzsch.

"This a kids' book?" said Larry.

"Some people mistakenly thought it was when it was published. But it's not. Not at all. It might be the deepest book Steinbeck wrote. It's about the seasons of life."

"Like they talk about in the Old Testament. Does it have the Lord in it?"

"Not by name. But it's a very spiritual book."

"Praise be," said Larry.

Anna watched him walk back toward his cell, book in hand.

She normally ate her lunch in the workroom because of the security hassle of returning to the jail, but she needed a break and decided to get some air. She left the facility and walked down past the parking lots to where the Anacostia Riverwalk Trail went along the Stadium-Armory Campus. The trail was wide enough to accommodate bikers and pedestrians, and she took it on foot, through the trees and along the river. About a mile and a half in, she crossed an elevated bridge that spanned a boatyard where colorful kayaks were stacked in numbers, and then she descended the sloping trail to the water's edge. She stood beneath the Sousa Bridge and looked across the river to its east bank.

When she'd first moved to Washington, she'd ride her bike down to the Anacostia via city streets because there was no trail. Men were often day-camped here, sitting on folding chairs, bottom-fishing for their supper, pulling perch and catfish out of the brackish water. The river, once polluted, was improving by then but still unclean. She wouldn't have eaten any fish that swam in it but she supposed the men knew what they were doing. They called her "Slim" and "baby" and offered her cheap beer from their coolers but were not at all threatening. She rarely saw locals like them here anymore.

It was young couples wearing Patagonia and pushing baby strollers, joggers in *Runner's World* gear. But they were part of the D.C. fabric now too.

Gulls swooped down and threw black shadows on the stanchions of the bridge. A slight wind came up and rippled the water. It was lovely here, still.

Her thoughts went to Donnell and his comments: "It's kind of everyone's fantasy, right? To have a new start."

She was not one of those who wanted to run away. She was into Washington. She liked dealing with the inmates and turning them on to books. Maybe it would not be her life's work but it was better than fine for now. And yet there was something missing in her overall day-to-day, particularly with Rick. Given his even temperament, burgeoning career, and good looks, she would find this difficult to explain to a friend. But then, she had few people in her life that she could truly confide in. It was strange that she had found it so easy to be with Michael Hudson and open up to him. Michael, with his gentle manner, his confidence, the stylish way he wore the cap on his head, his deep brown eyes.

"No," she said aloud, and then she shook her head, because what she was thinking was wrong.

Anna walked back toward the jail.

MICHAEL HUDSON loaded up a rack of clean glassware from out of the dishwasher, his earbuds in, his phone playing Backyard Band's *Street Antidote,* a go-go set he'd been listening to for the past hour. He lifted the rack, distributed its weight against his apron, and headed for the spiral stairs that led to the bar and dining room.

The kitchen had grown warmer as the spring progressed, and he was sweating, but he was in work shape and he was fine. As he neared the stairs, he was stopped by a pull on his T-shirt from behind. It was Blanca, the pizza-station cook, with her red-rinse hair and Raggedy Ann cheeks, oven scars wormed on her inner forearms. She was smiling. She stood on her toes, reached up, and removed one of Michael's earbuds. Now he was half listening to his go-go, half listening to the Spanish, horn-driven music that was blaring trebly from the Bluetooth speakers the crew had set up in the kitchen.

"What you want, Blanca?"

"Just bothering you, baby."

"Can't you see I'm busy?"

"Don't be so serious." She raised her arms and did some sort of abbreviated cha-cha move. "You want to dan'?"

"I'm on the clock. They don't pay me to *dan'*. But if they did, I'd dance you so hard your head would spin."

"I spin on you," she said. She turned to Maria, her friend in the kitchen, and winked. Both of them doubled over in laughter. Michael nearly blushed.

He headed up the stairs. Trying to negotiate the turns and watch his footing, he came upon Joe, who was descending. Joe gave Michael a short backfist in the groin as he passed.

"Good thing my hands are full, amigo," said Michael.

"I drop you like a tall tree," said Joe, and he gave Michael an air kiss.

In the hall leading to the bar, Michael smiled. Thinking, *I'm in.*

He had lunch at a two-top up in the empty top-floor dining room after the rush. He was eating and reading his book when Angelos Valis came out of the office, where he had been doing some paperwork.

"You got a minute?" said Angelos, taking a seat across from Michael.

"You fixin to give me my walking papers?"

"The opposite. Just wanted to tell you that you're doing a good job."

"So that means what? A raise?"

Angelos shook his head with theatrical regret. "Negative. Your raises are triggered by the D.C. minimum-wage laws. I told you that. But I would like to put you on our health-insurance plan. You'd have to contribute a small portion of your paycheck, but it's very reasonable, and the plan is solid. Do you have health insurance now?"

"No."

"Well, if you got sick or got in an accident or something, who'd pay the bills?"

His mother would step up, thought Michael, but he was too ashamed to say so.

"How much would I have to pay?" said Michael.

"I'll print the deal out for you so you can look it over."

"That costs y'all money," said Michael. "Why would you do it?"

"I talked it over with the owner. We like your performance and your work ethic. It's an incentive for you to stay with us. We want you to." Angelos stood from his chair. "I'll let you finish your lunch in peace."

Angelos went down the stairs. Michael began to read his book,

Northline. He couldn't stay away from the novel now or put it out of mind. Allison Johnson's story was coming to an end.

A GOOD detective has to have patience along with ambition. On Ornazian's fourth trip out to the house on Wagner Lane, early in the evening, Terry Kelly came home.

Terry parked his bright red Charger in front of his parents' house, got out of the car, and retrieved a laundry basket topped off with clothes from the backseat. Ornazian, three houses down the block, took photos of Terry, then watched him as he used his key to enter the house. Terry was muscular, with closely shaved hair and an unusually long face and wide forehead. He was tall. Ornazian put him at about six foot two.

Ornazian took photos of the car and used his fingers to spread them wide on the screen to ensure that he had gotten the tag numbers. The R/T badge was visible on the grille of the Charger, as were the dual scoops on the hood. Underneath was a V-8 Hemi. Ornazian remembered pricing out this model years ago. If the car had been purchased new, the father had dropped forty grand on a gift for his son. A lot of money, symbolic of his pride in a kid who had been accepted to a college where he was set to play D-1 ball on a scholarship. Ornazian could only imagine the father's disbelief when Terry started failing in school and then got busted on a distro beef. The old man's world must have imploded. The kid, now an adult, still drove the car, a laughing reminder of his steep fall.

Ornazian hit Thaddeus Ward up on his office phone.

"Ward Bonds," said the man himself.

"Like the character actor?"

"What do you want, Phil? I got no time for your nonsense."

"I found Terry Kelly. One of the guys who stole the Tiffany bracelet."

"And?"

"He came home to roost. I'm outside his father's house. I'm going to tail him and see where he goes."

"Don't get burned."

"Thanks, Dad. Actually, I don't have to hug him too close. He's driving a car so bright, I can see it from miles away. It's real subtle, like napalm dropping on a forest."

"Was the Vietnam reference for me?"

"I forgot to mention the Zippo lighter."

"You need a ride-along?"

"Sure. There's plenty of time for you to get out here. Terry's doing his laundry."

Ornazian gave Ward the address.

Three hours later, they were following the Charger out of the Washington metropolitan area and onto 270 North. They drove for over an hour, past Frederick, on to Route 15, then turned left off the highway to a two-lane that ran through a sparsely populated town called Hillville at the foot of the Catoctin Mountains. There, Terry Kelly went up a winding grade and turned into a gravel driveway that led to a house set back in a stand of pines.

TWENTY-TWO

THE FOLLOWING morning, Terry Kelly woke up to the sounds of his phone alarm and the hard-core thrash of a band called Storm. His housemates had downloaded the tune off a Maryland-based website that sold CDs, clothing, and other items that promoted white supremacy. If Terry had had any historical perspective, he might have noted that the music sounded very similar to that of first-wave D.C. punk groups like Minor Threat, albeit with racist lyrics. But he had no historical perspective. He merely had a headache.

The night before, Terry and his housemates, Richard Rupert and Tommy Getz, had drunk a case of beer and a bottle of Jack and smoked plentiful amounts of weed.

Richard put the music on first thing every morning. He said it got him motivated for his day. Terry sometimes wished that Richard would give it a rest. The music had sounded great last night, when they were torched and dancing with their shirts off, but the barking vocals and speedy guitars were grating at seven thirty a.m. Terry was a believer, but if pressed he would admit that white-nationalist rock lyrics were pretty much the same from song to song. Some young guy lamenting about old days he'd never actually experienced when jobs were plentiful for white people, before "others" arrived, fucked up the neighborhood with graffiti, gangs, and cheap labor, and ruined everything.

> Our grandfathers built this town
> Now it's been run to the ground
> But we're gonna stay and fight
> With one last chance to make things right!

Terry sat up on the edge of the bed and rubbed his temples. Unlike the guy shouting those lines, he had to go to work. So did his friends. The three of them had jobs in towns outside of Frederick. Terry was a stocker in a small grocery store in Walkersville. Richard and Tommy were in an auto-body shop in Monrovia.

They had met when all of them worked as body men in a garage in Gaithersburg, a Maryland suburb north of D.C. Terry supplied them with marijuana that he was moving in quantity with some guys he had befriended out of the Cherry Hill Road area in eastern Montgomery County. Richard and Tommy were polite with Terry but kept their distance. Later, when Terry got busted and told them about his situation, he found out why. They couldn't abide white people who hung out with blacks. They told him that his troubles were *because* of the blacks. Blacks had no honor. They were inferior to whites in every way. Come court time, they would turn on Terry. Blacks and whites didn't belong together. Terry needed to choose a side.

After he flipped on his former friends and drew probation

rather than time, Terry got some threatening texts and phone messages and began to see that Richard and Tommy were right. He'd been misguided. A white man could only trust whites.

Terry shaved off his beard, which he used to get shaped up at one of the many black barbershops in Silver Spring. He began to hang tight with Richard and Tommy. They took him along to white-nationalist meetings outside Baltimore and to larger events, picnics, rallies, and concerts, up in Harrisburg, Pennsylvania, where the Keystone State Skinheads got their start. Gradually, Terry began to see the truth. White genocide was real. He told himself that he didn't hate black people, but he and his friends had to do something to protect the true American way of life that had been under siege for far too long.

When Richard got caught stealing tools from the shop in Gaithersburg and was fired, Terry and Tommy quit in an act of solidarity, and the three of them decided to rent a place up in Frederick County, where they could be among their own kind. Richard and Tommy got body work and Terry snagged a job in a local grocery chain. They rented a house together in Hillville, a secluded mountain community off Route 15 that was heavily populated by whites. There they worked day jobs as a cover for their more lucrative activities, which included all varieties of theft, dealing marijuana to coworkers, and selling cut-down Lean to gullible white kids they trolled on Facebook and Instagram. They called them Eight Milers: whites who wanted to be black. Like white people who adopted black kids, they were race traitors, and they deserved to get fucked.

Terry dressed, left his small bedroom, and walked out into the kitchen/living area. It had a table, where they ate, and a TV that got its signal from a dish mounted on the roof. Richard and

Tommy were at the table in their work clothes, finishing their cereal, about to head out to the shop. Like Terry, they were tall, six foot plus. Richard had the fancy haircut, shaved on the sides and full on top. His unbuttoned shirt revealed his ink, the usual lightning bolts and number symbols. Tommy kept his hair shorn to the scalp. Both of them were strong.

Terry had some cereal too, and then the three of them left the house. Richard secured the front and rear doors with a barrel lock and a dead bolt. All the windows were fixed with high-impact plastic burglar bars. Richard and Tommy had their guns and other valuables in a large framed-out box under a floor cutout in Richard's bedroom. Terry kept a pistol under the front seat of his car. He was aware of the risk of having an unlicensed gun, but the threat of the Cherry Hill Road boys was still in his head.

They walked to their vehicles: Terry's Charger, Richard's lifted Cherokee, and Tommy's Silverado, parked in the gravel drive amid tall pines. They punched each other's fists by way of good-bye. Terry felt a swell of pride. He was one of them. He had always felt apart, in his private school, on the baseball team, and, looking back on it, whenever he was riding with those gator-baits who he thought were his friends. For the first time in his life, with Richard and Tommy, he felt like he was a part of something. He belonged.

They drove down the winding grade to the town: a sparsely populated strip of houses, a gas station, a church, and a failed general store. They followed Hillville Road to Route 15 and headed off to their daily jobs.

* * *

PHIL ORNAZIAN and Thaddeus Ward sat in Ward's Crown Vic behind the shuttered general store, waiting. They had rolled the dice, hoping that the three vehicles they had seen outside the tan-siding house in the pines the night before would be headed off to work the following morning. They had met up at Ward's bail-bond office before dawn.

A traffic alert on Ornazian's phone had told him that a tractor-trailer overturn on 270 North had shut down the highway, so they headed toward Baltimore in darkness and caught Route 70 in the direction of Frederick.

"They call this the Heroin Highway," said Ward as they hit 70 East. "State police randomly stop cars with West Virginia plates. Those boys make their pickup in Baltimore and drive the product back to their home state. Lots of heroin transactions in the parking lot of that Walmart in Mount Airy too."

"How do you know all this?" said Ornazian.

"Fella I worked with in Four D, name of Burnside. Moved out to West Virginia after he left the force. You know how police do. Burnside took his tier-two retirement and put the big city in his rearview. But he never stopped being a cop. Burnside knows what goes on in all these towns up here, Maryland, West Virginia…Pennsetucky too."

"Did you ask him about Hillville?"

Ward nodded. "He says Hillville is the meth capital of Maryland. Told me to mind myself up here, 'cause these Hillvillies don't take kindly to strangers they think might be law. 'Specially the federal type."

"We're not law," said Ornazian.

"Who don't know *that*?" said Ward.

Coming off Route 15 onto Hillville Road, they saw a sign in a plowed field announcing a pending housing development. On the sign was spray-painted the words *Get out.*

They had arrived in a kind of town center—a church, a gas station and small market, and widely spaced houses. Farther along, the houses were smaller and in disrepair. Some had weed-ridden cars, trucks, and farm equipment in their yards. BEWARE OF DOG signs and multiple satellite dishes were common. They came to a shuttered general store at the foot of the Catoctin Mountains. There the road wound up toward the house where Terry Kelly stayed with his friends. Ward pulled the Vic around back of the store, put it nose-out so they could see the road, and cut the engine.

Back behind the store was a semicircle of houses so small they were nearly shacks. In the center of the semicircle was a rusted-out jungle gym and swing set. One of the houses had an open, unhinged front door. Another had windows spray-painted black.

"Meth pads," said Ward.

An hour past dawn, the Charger came down the hill, followed by a boxy Jeep with oversize tires and a Chevy half-ton truck.

"That's them," said Ornazian.

"The new Klansmen."

"More like wannabe Nazis."

"What's the difference?"

"Their playbook is *Mein Kampf.* They carved the number fourteen into the Weitzmans' dining-room table."

"And that means what?"

"Fourteen words. The white-nationalist slogan. 'I am a coward and a loser and I blame my failure on other people.'"

Ward counted it out on his fingers. "That's fifteen words."

"See? These guys could fuck up a wet dream. Let's go to their house."

Ward drove up the hill. He passed the house with its now empty driveway and kept going for another two miles. The road ended at a county watershed area with NO TRESPASSING signs mounted on a closed gate.

"I don't like it," said Ward. "Only way out is back down that hill."

"Always with the negative waves, Moriarty."

"Now you're losing me, man."

Ward made a three-point turn and drove down the grade. They went by a ramshackle home set improbably on a steep hill, where three young men sat on a porch and hard-eyed them as they passed. Ward continued on and parked on the shoulder of the road, just a bit north of the tan rambler set in the stand of pines.

"We're out of the sight lines of the other houses," said Ward.

Ornazian looked around at the surrounding woods and nodded. "Let's see what we've got."

They went to the trunk of the Crown Vic and opened it. They gloved their hands but did not use stockings on their faces. Ward checked his Glock, holstered it, and left his shotgun where it lay. Ornazian slid the .38 into his dip and reached for his retractable baton.

"You won't need that today," said Ward. He unzipped a duffel bag and extracted a twenty-five-inch-long Blackhawk special-ops entry ram, gripping it by its top handle. There were also handles on both sides of the batterer.

"You police love your toys," said Ornazian.

"This is a nice tool right here. It weighs thirty pounds. Even you could handle it."

"Why's it got three handles? You only have two hands."

"It's designed so right-handed dudes and left-handed dudes can use it. Dumbass."

"I wish you wouldn't call me that. I'm a little sensitive right now."

"Is it your time of month?"

"I hate when you blame all of my emotions on that."

They looked around once more, crossed the roughly paved road, and walked to the back of the house.

"I don't hear no dogs," said Ward.

The house backed to a hill of weed and boulders. The rear door was up three concrete steps, where there was a small landing. Ornazian tried the door to negative effect, then stepped back as Ward stood before it, feet planted firmly, and gripped the forward handle of the ram with his left hand, one of the rear handles with his right. He swung the ram into the jamb, and the door opened, its frame splintering cleanly. Ward placed the battering ram on the concrete landing and both of them stepped into the house.

They were in a kitchen that smelled of garbage. A sack of it was full and open in a plastic basket, and there were dirty dishes, cups, and silverware piled in the sink. A cheaply made dining table outside the kitchen held four chairs. There was an open living area with a couch, cable-spool table, recliner, and wide-screen television.

On the cable-spool table sat an open laptop, many empty beer cans, a bong, a bag of buds, rolling papers, plastic lighters, and an ashtray full of cigarette butts and roaches. Posters showing Aryan faces and accompanying slogans were thumbtacked haphazardly to the walls. WE HAVE A RIGHT TO EXIST. FIGHTING TO TAKE BACK OUR COMMUNITIES ONE STREET AT A TIME. OUR FUTURE BELONGS TO US.

Ornazian scanned the posters, the words, the bold fonts and art deco–style images typically found on Ayn Rand book covers.

He went to the laptop and looked at the site that was still up on the screen, a music label promoting its product and its racist ideology. Ornazian hit one of the songs on a downloadable list, something called "When the Righteous Day Comes" by a band named Blood Duty. Growls and red-needle guitars filled the room.

"Even their music sucks," said Ornazian.

"Turn that shit off," said Ward. "What we're looking for ain't out here. Let's go to the bedrooms."

There were three of them. Ornazian and Ward worked each room together. They opened drawers and shoeboxes, tossed closets, sliced up mattresses. In the largest bedroom, the last one they entered, boxes of a prescription medication, a combination of promethazine and codeine, were stacked on a small throw rug in a corner. Next to the stacks, lined up, sat bottles of NyQuil. Christopher Perry, the kid from Northeast, had been right. These guys were cutting their Lean with over-the-counter cold medicine.

"Fuck is that mess?" said Ward.

"The latest trash high."

"In my day, the burnouts huffed glue out of paper bags."

"Same idea."

Ornazian and Ward searched the room and found no Tiffany bracelet. There was no jewelry at all and no cash.

"Nothing," said Ornazian.

"You think they already offed it?"

"I don't know."

"Let's get out of here, man."

Out in the living room, Ornazian said, "Hold up."

He ripped the posters off the walls and violently overturned the cable-spool table. He grabbed a chair and threw it into the wall-mounted television set, cracking its screen. Then he unbuttoned his fly, pulled out his pecker, and urinated on the couch.

"You finished?" said Ward. "Or you about to take a shit in their beds too?"

"That was for my kids."

Driving back through the town of Hillville, Ward turned to Ornazian.

"Guess we'll have to come back and do it the tried-and-true way."

"I guess we will."

"They'll be on alert now. Seein as how you trashed the shit outta their spot."

"You're the one who broke their doorframe."

"I ain't piss on it, though."

"True."

"We can come back," said Ward, "but not with my car."

"I'll score the SS."

"Where'd that Impala come from?"

"Man named Berhanu, deals in hacks. Has a little garage in an alley off Taylor, near Kansas Avenue, in Petworth."

"You trust him?"

"He's straight."

"Can you get Hudson?"

"I'll get him."

"He didn't seem too happy about being with us the last time."

"He wasn't," said Ornazian. "But he'll come around."

TWENTY-THREE

MICHAEL HUDSON returned home from his day shift at the District Line and let Brandy out into the backyard to do her business. Back in the empty lot, where the east–west portion of the alley came to a T, the man named Woods sat on a crate. Woods had lost a foot in Iraq after an IED detonated under his Humvee. For that, he received seven hundred dollars a month in compensation. Woods had yet to find work in D.C.

"Hudson," said Woods, giving Michael a two-fingered salute.

"Woods," said Michael with a nod.

After Brandy defecated, she dragged her butt across the weedy yard and then came to the back steps and whined. Michael picked her up in his arms and carried her upstairs. Brandy slept at the foot of Michael's bed while he finished *Northline*. He had been waiting for some quiet time alone to finish the novel.

In the story, Allison Johnson has sought out the disfigured young man Dan Mahony who disappeared from her life for weeks and is holed up, hermit-like, in his small house. He lets her in, and, after some gentle prodding on her part, he reveals the details of his troubled past and the source of his depression. While he showers, she cleans his house thoroughly in an act of kindness and suggests that Dan and his dog walk her to the restaurant where she works. She's trying to draw Dan Mahony back out into the world. At the same time, Allison, cautious around men after a lifetime of abuse, is letting down her guard.

> *"I'd like that," he said and stood up. He walked to a closet and got his coat. The girl put on her coat, hat, and gloves and they walked out into the yard. It was dark as they went down Seventh Street towards the casinos and the downtown lights. Dan Mahony couldn't take control of her, she thought to herself, he could barely take control of himself. So as she walked, she felt all right with him there. Her hand fell next to his and she took it in hers and held it.*

Michael put down the book for a moment, then read that last sentence again. Then he read on. In the penultimate chapter, Allison, Dan Mahony, and his dog go to Nevada's Black Rock Desert, camp out, and sleep under the stars in the bed of Dan's old pickup. In the end, two damaged people have found refuge, healing, and hope in each other's arms.

Michael rubbed at the cover of the book, then placed it spine-out on the shelf next to his Elmore Leonard novels, *Hombre* and *Valdez Is Coming*. His library had begun to grow.

He took a shower, dressed in fresh clothes, and had an early dinner with his mother. Then he walked northeast, out of Columbia Heights, into Park View.

* * *

MICHAEL WAS standing near the entrance to the rec center on Warder Street, hoping that Anna Byrne would appear. He didn't want to lurk too close to her house. It was a long shot, but he knew she rode her bike in the evenings. Sure enough, soon she was pedaling toward him on her machine. Upon seeing him, she slowed to a roll and braked with one foot. She was surprised, but the look on her face was not displeased.

"Michael…"

"I was in the neighborhood."

"Okay."

"Actually, I *walked* to your neighborhood. I was hoping to get up with you."

"Is something wrong?"

"No. I just wanted to see you."

She stared at him and he didn't look away.

"I'm about to go for a ride," she said.

"I get it."

"No, listen. Give me an hour. We can meet up when I come back. If you don't mind me being sweaty."

"I don't mind. Where?"

"You remember that beer garden on Georgia?"

"Next to that bookstore. At Morton."

"One hour," said Anna. "I'll see you there."

Michael clocked her as she headed downtown. When she left his sight, he walked through the rec center gates and had a seat on the bleachers by the field. Watched some dudes playing a soccer game; looked like they were serious. He could tell they were El Salvadoran by their features. Since he'd been on the job, he'd learned to distinguish the countries of origin of the folks in the kitchen. It was cool to know who your neighbors were and where they'd come from. They were D.C. too.

PHIL ORNAZIAN stood outside a four-car garage in an alley behind Taylor Street, near Kansas Avenue. He counted out cash and handed it over to Berhanu, the man with the tight curls who dealt in hacks.

"That do it?" said Ornazian.

"I'll have the SS ready for you," said Berhanu. "You put a little wear on the front end last time."

"That's what the extra is for. We had to go off-road, unfortunately. I hope it wasn't bad."

Berhanu gave a short wave of his hand. "Minor undercarriage work. You covered it."

Donnie, the alcoholic mechanic, came out of the garage and lit a cigarette. He made brief eye contact with Ornazian but their interaction went no further.

"Mr. Personality," said Ornazian.

Berhanu shrugged. "He's good with a wrench."

"I'll need that Impala soon."

"Fine, but I won't be reachable at night. It's Holy Week."

"Understood."

"Are you planning on going to church?"

"Sure." It was a soft lie. With everything he'd been managing, Ornazian had nearly forgotten about Orthodox Easter. He was too ashamed to admit this to Berhanu.

"Ciao, Phil."

"Ciao. I'll hit you up."

They shook hands. Ornazian walked to his Ford amid the harsh barking of alley dogs.

MICHAEL SAT across from Anna at a picnic table on the patio of the Midlands. She had washed up in the bathroom and let her hair down. She wore a locally designed Rapteez T-shirt over bike leggings. Her Cannondale leaned against the bar's chain-link fence. She was having a lager and Michael was drinking a ginger ale. Several dogs roamed the area, their owners hanging with friends. An employee was barbecuing ribs as a Sturgill Simpson song came through the house speakers, the man singing in a rich baritone about a promise he'd made.

"Never thought I'd hear a country song playing in this neighborhood," said Michael.

"Country's just one of the things this guy is," said Anna. "Anyway, they'll probably play GoldLink or something like that next. All kinds of people patronize this place. You've got to serve your clientele."

"I reckon."

"You don't like it?"

"I don't stress on things I can't change." Michael sipped his drink. "All this new stuff happened quick, though. I wasn't locked up for all that long."

"Everything happens quickly now. The hands on the clock are spinning faster. Don't you feel it?"

"Yes. What's that mean, though? That you should slow yourself down and enjoy it? Or pack in as much as you can 'cause time is short?"

"I don't know what it means," said Anna. "I go to work every day and try to do something positive. I don't have grand ambitions. Make a living, make a little impact on someone's life, if I can. That's the most anyone can hope for, I think."

"Small kindnesses. Like in the book."

"Which book?"

"The one you gave me. *Northline.* Every time something horrible happened to that girl, over and over again, when it seemed like she was too far gone to ever come back, someone did something nice for her. Wasn't anything major. But it made a difference. She learned. Eventually, she ended up helping that dude with the scars the same way."

"What did that tell you?"

"The bad in the world, it can keep coming at you. But one small act of kindness can overpower the dark."

"I loved that book."

"So did I. Thank you for giving it to me. And for everything you did when I was in the jail. You changed my life."

Their eyes locked. Anna blushed.

"What?" said Michael.

"Nothing. It was my pleasure."

Michael held her gaze. "How is it for you?" he said.

"How's what?"

"Are you happy?"

She hesitated, because how she answered would have implications for them both. Her heart wanted many different things. But she knew what was right.

"I don't think I'm all that different from anybody else," she said. "I definitely have a lot to be thankful for. So I'm pretty happy, I guess. Most of the time I am."

"With your man, I mean."

"I know what you were asking. Yes."

Michael nodded. He needed to know.

On impulse, Anna reached across the table and laid her hand over Michael's. The feeling was electric. She kept it there, looking into his eyes. Then she slowly withdrew it.

They sat there as Anna finished her beer, comfortable with each other in the gathering dark.

SHE WALKED her bike up the hill toward Warder and he walked beside her. They said good-bye a block from her house. She watched him as he turned the corner at Princeton and headed west.

Michael took his time walking home. He had received a text and answered it. Now he needed to think.

The black Edge was parked on Sherman, right in front of his mother's house. Michael opened the door and got into the passenger bucket.

"Michael."

"Told you I'd meet you up the street."

"This was the only spot available."

"Say what you came here for."

"I've got another job for you," said Ornazian.

"What makes you think I'd do it?"

"Me and Thaddeus are about to do a home invasion out in the country. These guys stole some valuable jewelry from a house party. Raped the teenage girl who lived there. They're white supremacists. Bad people all the way around."

"Don't play me, Phil."

"I need you. You drove the shit out of that Impala when it counted. I don't know anybody who can do what you do."

"Always on the hustle. What you gonna do now, threaten to send me back to jail?"

"I don't think I have to."

Michael stared ahead. "When?"

"Soon."

"Don't come near my mother's house again. Hear?"

Michael got out of the Ford. Ornazian pulled off the curb and drove toward Petworth. He wanted to see his sons before they went to sleep.

TWENTY-FOUR

THEY DROVE up the graded road at night, Michael at the wheel of the SS, Ornazian beside him. Thaddeus Ward was in the backseat. The headlights were off. Michael navigated by the light of the moon. They passed the house in the pines, and Ornazian told him to keep going, and then, after a hundred yards, he told him to turn around. Nearing the house, Ornazian instructed Michael to pull over and cut the engine.

"Wait," said Ward. "Back it into the woods instead."

"What if we get stuck?" said Ornazian.

"It hasn't rained for a week," said Ward. "Ground's packed hard. We'll be fine."

Michael did it. The Impala was partially hidden by oak and scrub pine, its nose out. They could see the house clearly. The curtains were drawn, and lights were on inside. Only the Cherokee and Silverado were in the gravel driveway. There was no Charger.

"Where's our boy?" said Ward.

"Who knows?" said Ornazian. "Still at work? It doesn't matter. We don't want him, we only want what they stole."

"We could wait till Kelly gets back," said Ward.

"There's no telling when or if he's coming back tonight. I don't think we should wait."

"Okay," said Ward, trying to think of all the possibilities. "They know someone broke into their house. They'll be on alert."

"What's your point?"

"We have to go in hard. I'll use the ram and you need to cover them with the shotgun."

"Right." Ornazian clipped a two-way radio to his belt and handed its mate to Michael. "Stay on channel eleven."

"Like last time."

"Kelly's tall with a long face and a broad forehead," said Ornazian, speaking to Michael. "If he comes back to the house, remember, you're with us. You know what that means."

Michael said nothing. But he understood what Ornazian was saying. He was expected to back them up.

"You done speechifying?" said Ward.

"Not yet," said Ornazian. "I just want to remind everyone that these are bad people. They drugged and assaulted a girl. They'd just as soon see you swinging from a tree as look at you, Thaddeus."

"You don't need to gin me up," said Ward. "I was a kid in Washington in the fifties. My father was a veteran of World War Two, a taxpayer, and a straight citizen, and still, I heard him get called a nigger many times. Do you know what that does to a boy who looks up to his father? My mother worked for the federal government, but come Easter, she couldn't buy a hat or a dress in one of those downtown department stores or walk into the Garfinckel's on Fourteenth Street and spend

226

the money she'd earned. That is, until 1968. That's when we burned Fourteenth Street to the ground. So, yeah, I know who these people are. It's you who don't know. You too, Hudson. Either you never took the time to learn your history or you forgot. It's the forgetting that allows trash like them to come back.

"This past year been the darkest time I can remember. But I did smile once. When that white-supremacist dude came to town and someone just up and coldcocked him right in the face. This is *Washington*, man. The percentages are down, but it's still a black city. Always gonna be a black city to me. Some white boy comes into D.C. and starts talking that filth, he's gonna get his punk ass handed to him real quick.

"So there ain't no need for you to get my blood going, Phil. I got a daughter. She's more accomplished than any of these people will ever be, and still, in their eyes, she's mud."

"I have kids too."

"Yeah, your black kids. You white folk get all self-righteous when you taste a little of what we've been swallowing for almost five hundred years."

"I know what side I'll be fighting on if the race war comes," said Ornazian.

"So do I," said Ward. "But before we get all apocalyptic, why don't we just handle what we got right here tonight?"

"Y'all finished?" said Michael.

"I reckon," said Ward.

Michael released the trunk lid as Ornazian disabled the dome light of the car's interior then opened his door. He and Ward got out of the car and went around to the open trunk. Ward had transferred many items from his Crown Vic to the Impala when they picked him up in the parking lot behind his shop. They had already removed the trunk's light. Ward took a mini Maglite from his multipocketed jacket, turned it on, and put its ass end in his mouth. They gloved their hands and worked by that light.

Ward checked the load on his Glock, holstered it behind his back, and put several sets of plastic restraints of varying lengths in his pockets. Ornazian broke open the wheel of the .38 Special, saw rounds fitted in its chambers, and slid the revolver into the dip of his jeans. He took the Remington 12-gauge out of its blanket and hefted it.

"Tipped slugs," said Ward. "Don't rack it yet. They'll piss their drawers when they hear that sound."

Ward unzipped the duffel bag, brought out the battering ram, and laid it on the floor of the trunk. He then opened a case and produced something that looked like a gun but was not. Ornazian knew exactly what it was. He had bought one himself on the black market. Ward found an extra cartridge in the case and fixed it to the end of the butt.

"What's that?"

"Speed load," said Ward.

Ward slipped the weapon into a plastic holster and clipped the rig to his belt. Then he and Ornazian pulled stockings down over their faces. Before Ward picked up the ram and closed the trunk, Ornazian grabbed the retractable steel baton and walked it around to the driver's side of the SS. He handed it to Michael Hudson.

"You might need this," said Ornazian. Michael put the baton on the seat beside him.

Ward was standing next to Ornazian, squinting, looking across the road at the house.

"Can you see them?" said Ornazian, whose night vision was poor.

"No," said Ward. "But I'm guessin they ain't watching TV. You saw to that."

"Back door?"

Ward nodded. "We busted it in good. They probably haven't had time to fortify it yet."

"Let's go."

They crossed the road, walking low, avoiding the gravel driveway. They went to the side of the house and pressed themselves against it. They allowed themselves to calm their nerves and steady their breath, and then they went to the back of the house, where Ward ascended the concrete steps to the back-door landing. He cautiously peered into the kitchen. Ornazian came up behind him in a crouch, giving him room to make his play. Ward looked at him once, held up two fingers, and nodded, then gripped the ram by its top and left-side handle. He swung it into the jamb and the door crashed open. Ward dropped the ram onto the landing and drew his Glock. Both of them stepped into the house.

"Don't nobody move," said Ward.

Richard Rupert and Tommy Getz, startled, were seated at the small table. There was a semiautomatic on it. Richard stood and reached for it as the invaders entered the kitchen. He stopped at Ward's command and the sound of the rack of the shotgun in Ornazian's grip. Tommy had not gotten up from his seat. His hands were visibly shaking.

Ward jacked a round into the Glock as he moved forward. Ornazian leveled the 12-gauge on the young men. The one who was standing had the pretty-boy haircut, shaved sides, long on top. The seated one's hair was down to the scalp. Their shirts were off and they were barefoot and wearing jeans. They were both cock-strong but had no lines or beard shadows on their faces. Ornazian had to remind himself that they were violent men. They looked like kids.

"Put your hands up," said Ward.

They did it. There was hate and embarrassment in the standing one's eyes.

"Say your names," said Ward.

"Fuck you is my name," said Richard Rupert.

Ward stepped forward so fast he blurred. He swung the barrel of the Glock, and Richard went down to the floor. He rubbed at his jaw and worked it. Soon it would be swollen and blue.

"Mind your tongue and stand up," said Ward. "Now, what's your name?"

"Richard."

"You?"

"T-T-Tom," said the other.

We have a stutterer, thought Ornazian. He knew what Ward would do with that. It was his show.

"Take the rest of your clothes off," said Ward. "Not just your blue jeans. Everything. Your panties too."

Richard began to take off his clothes. Tommy Getz hesitated.

"You too, T-T-T-Tom."

RICHARD AND Tommy were cuffed to the table chairs, hands and feet secured by plastic ties. They were naked and sweating. The room smelled of their rank perspiration.

"Y'all motherfuckas stink," said Ward.

"What do you want?" said Richard.

"We're here for the Tiffany bracelet. The one you stole from that house in Potomac. Don't waste my time and act like you don't know what I'm talking about."

"I got rid of it," said Richard.

"I don't believe you."

"You already tossed our house. That was you who broke in, right? So you know it's not here anymore."

"Yeah? Where's the money you made from the sale?"

"I put it in the fucking bank."

"You're too stupid to have a bank account."

Richard stared defiantly into Ward's eyes. Tommy looked down at his lap.

"Tom," said Ward. "Look at me." Tommy looked at Ward. "Where's the bracelet?"

"Don't say nothin to him, Tommy," said Richard.

Ward drew the Taser from its holster. He flicked off its safety and stood directly in front of Tommy.

"The company made some improvements on this model right here," said Ward. "Lawmen complained that it wasn't powerful enough. Used to be twenty thousand volts, so they upped it to fifty. The darts were smooth, but now they got barbs on 'em, like little fishhooks. According to a video I watched, if the Taser is sighted just below the sternum, the lower dart kind of harpoons the genitals."

Ward sighted the Taser. A red dot appeared below Tommy's sternum. "That's where the top electrode gonna hit. The bottom one will hit your privates."

"Don't," said Tommy.

"Fifty thousand volts to your p-p-penis and scrotum, Tom. You gonna feel that up into your spine. If I hold down the trigger long enough, it's gonna burn you too. Leave you—what's that word…nonfunctional. Nerve damage, all that. You ain't never gonna be the same down there again."

Tears broke and ran down Tommy's face.

"Leave him alone," said Richard.

"Okay," said Ward.

He stepped over to Richard Rupert. He trained the laser on the area of Richard's solar plexus where a tiny swastika had been inked into his skin. "It was you who raped that girl. *Wasn't* it, Richard? You don't look like much, but I'm guessing you fancy yourself a real rooster."

Richard held Ward's stare.

"Where's the bracelet, Richard?" said Ward.

"It's up in your fat ass."

Ward triggered the Taser, igniting its gas cartridge. Two conductive wires shot out of the muzzle. The electrified darts found their marks and invaded Richard Rupert's nerves. His muscles contracted violently. He bucked and writhed in his chair. His hands flopped in their cuffs and he toppled over, convulsing, as the smell of burned hair and flesh permeated the room. Tommy Getz turned his head and vomited.

"Enough," said Ornazian.

Ward laid the Taser down on the floor and walked back over to Tommy.

"Now you need to tell it, Tom."

* * *

MICHAEL HUDSON'S eyes were on the house in the pines when headlights came up the road. He watched as a car, looked like a Dodge from the lamps, slowed and pulled into the gravel drive-way. Had to be a V-8 from the sound coming out the pipes.

Michael picked up the two-way and keyed it.

"Come in, Number One," said Michael.

"It's me. What's going on?"

"We got company. Looks like our man."

"We're almost done here," said Ornazian. "Handle it."

Michael dropped the radio on the seat beside him and picked up the steel baton.

AFTER TOMMY had given it up, Ornazian went to Richard's bed-room and moved the boxes of promethazine, codeine, and NyQuil that were stacked in the corner. He then picked up a throw rug to find a cutout in the hardwood floor. He crouched down and pulled on a ring set in a grooved-out portion of the floor. The cutout came up, revealing a framed-out box below.

In the box were an automatic, a revolver, several pieces of jewelry in a paper bag, a rubber-banded stack of cash, and a robin's-egg-blue box marked TIFFANY AND CO. Inside that box was the diamond-and-platinum bracelet.

They had missed the stash when they tossed the bedroom the first time around. It had been here, under the stacked in-gredients of the Lean.

Ornazian pocketed all of the jewelry, the bracelet, and the cash in his tan Kühl jacket. He ejected the magazine of a nine-millimeter Beretta and removed the bullets from the revolver and put those in his jacket as well.

He went back out to the living area to scoop up Ward. It was time to go.

TERRY KELLY noticed the car across the road, its front end jutting out of the woods, as he got out of his Charger. Looked like an old Chevy, maybe an Impala. A police package car, or Feds, maybe. There were no residents close by, and there wasn't any good reason for anyone to be parked in those woods.

Terry knew what Richard would say if he went into the house and told him and Tommy about the car: *Dumbass. Why didn't you check it out?*

Terry reached under the driver's seat and found his gun, a nine-millimeter Beretta he had bought on the street. He pulled back on the receiver and eased a round into the chamber. He snicked off the safety, slid the gun into the side pocket of his jacket, and walked across the road.

He went to the car. The night was dark but he could see that there was no one inside the vehicle and as his eyes adjusted he made out its make and model. It was indeed an Impala, the muscled-out nineties version of the SS. Terry walked into the stand of scrub pine to the rear of the car and examined the animal badge on the trunk's lid, the chrome pipes. He heard footsteps. His heart beat hard in his chest.

"Don't move," said a voice behind him.

Terry turned quickly and in that motion drew the Beretta from his side pocket and pointed it at the man standing before him, just three feet away. In the darkness he saw a tall, bearded man, nearly featureless in the dim light, holding a metal rod in his hand.

Though he held a gun, Terry felt the blood drain from his face.

"I don't want to die," said Terry, a quiver in his voice.

"Who said anything about dyin?"

"They sent you here to kill me, didn't they?" said Terry. "Isn't that right?"

"Who?"

"The Cherry Hill Road boys."

"Ain't nobody send me here. Toss that gun aside so we can talk."

"I can't do that," said Terry.

Michael Hudson looked at Terry Kelly. He wasn't hard. He was a stupid, confused kid. Michael had been in juvenile lockup and been incarcerated as an adult. He knew enough to see that this boy was weak.

"Do what I say," said Michael.

"I *can't*," said Terry.

Michael swung the steel baton. It struck Terry in the temple, and he lost his legs. Terry fell to the ground in a heap of dead-weight.

Michael tossed the gun into the woods. He got down on his knees and felt the blood on Terry Kelly's face.

I'm a murderer, thought Michael.

I killed a man.

* * *

IN THE living room, Ornazian told Ward that he had found what they'd come for. Richard was still in the toppled-over chair, conscious but disoriented. His genitals were burned and there was some blood where Ward had pulled out the barbs. He had voided his bowels. Ward had poured water on his face, but he was white as milk.

Ward told Tommy to let the incident go. Warned him what would happen if they went back to the house in Potomac or tried to retaliate in any way.

"Do you understand me?"

"Yes."

Ornazian and Ward left them there, bound to their chairs.

Outside the house, they crossed the road to the Impala and found Michael seated on the ground beside Terry Kelly.

"He's dead," said Michael.

"Put your light on him," said Ornazian to Ward.

Ward trained the mini Mag on Terry as Ornazian got down on his haunches and pressed his index and middle fingers to the carotid artery in the young man's neck. Then he found a bottle of water in the trunk and wet Terry's lips and poured some of it on his bloodied forehead and temple.

"He's not dead," said Ornazian. "I'm guessing you concussed him, but his pulse is running strong. He should be all right."

"We just gonna leave him here?" said Michael.

"He's lying on a soft bed of pine needles. When he wakes up, he'll go over to the house and cut his friends loose." Ornazian cupped his hand around Michael's biceps. "Listen, you did good."

"*Fuck* you, man," said Michael, pulling his arm away.

They drove off the mountain in silence. At Route 15,

Michael headed in the direction of D.C. Ornazian cracked a window to get some air. He was sickened by what they'd done.

"You don't look so good," said Michael.

"I'm fine," said Ornazian.

"Yeah? What'd you do to those guys in that house?"

"We got what we came for," said Ward.

"That's all that matters?" said Michael.

"Don't get all high and mighty, young man," said Ward.

"After tonight," said Michael, "I don't want nothin to do with y'all. Threaten me all you want. I'd rather go to prison than be with people like you."

"But you're still gonna take your cut," said Ward.

Michael's face was grim in the dashboard light.

TWENTY-FIVE

SYDNEY HAD prepared a large breakfast of bacon, eggs, sausage, beans, and mushrooms after Ornazian had woken up just past noon. It was what she called a Full English. He sat at their kitchen table eating ravenously, washing the meal down with juice and coffee.

The dogs, Whitey and Blue, were following Sydney around the kitchen, hoping for scraps. She commanded them to sit, and when they complied, she gave them each half a strip of bacon.

"You're spoiling them," said Ornazian.

"I'm spoiling *you*," said Sydney. "What time did you get in last night?"

"I don't know. It was pretty late. That's why I slept in. When did Gregg and Vic go to their playdate?"

"Well before you got up."

"I've got some running around to do today. Maybe we can all go out tonight. Get some fried chicken and crab cakes at that place on Upshur."

"The boys would love that," she said.

He went up to his office on the porch, made a couple of

phone calls, then showered, dressed, and loaded his daypack. Down on the first floor, Sydney was picking up toys, balls, and all varieties of plastic weapons. She walked Ornazian to the front door. They kissed. He felt a stirring and he kissed her again, deeply, his hand on the flat of her back.

"Later?" he said.

"Perhaps."

"You're smoking hot. You know that, don't you?"

"You just like me."

"That I do."

"Are you done with all the nonsense with Thaddeus?"

"Yes. I'm done."

"Maybe we can go back to our normal life now."

"That's the plan," he said.

He got into his Ford, parked on Taylor Street, and drove out to Potomac, Maryland, the Tiffany bracelet in his daypack on the seat beside him.

ORNAZIAN SAT at the kitchen table of the Weitzman residence, counting cash. After Ornazian had phoned him, Leonard Weitzman had gone to his bank and withdrawn twenty-five thousand dollars and placed it in a manila envelope. Now he dropped it on the table. Also on the table was the Tiffany box that held the bracelet and the jewelry that had been in the paper bag: a string of pearls, a couple of rings set with precious stones, and a pair of diamond earrings.

"We're good," said Ornazian, sliding the envelope into his daypack.

"What about the other items you retrieved?" said Weitzman, referring to the jewelry. He was seated at the table, wearing a pullover with the Congressional Country Club coat of arms, crossed gold clubs over the Capitol Dome, sewn on its breast.

"I'm throwing them in," said Ornazian. "If there's nothing else, I'll be on my way."

"There is one thing," said Weitzman. "I got a call from a man named Hanrahan. He says you spoke to his son, who apparently attended the party that night. You told the kid you'd go to the headmaster of his school if he didn't give you some information."

"That's right."

"Hanrahan threatened me with legal action."

"Is there a question?"

"I asked you not to involve any of the kids or their parents."

"You got what you wanted, didn't you?"

"Yes."

"You'll find a way to deal with Hanrahan," said Ornazian.

"I didn't mean to sound ungrateful. You did good work for me."

Ornazian stood. Weitzman offered his hand and Ornazian shook it, accepting the compliment without comment. He looked through the kitchen windows to the deck, where Lisa sat on a cushioned bench. She was staring out into the yard, ashing a cigarette onto her jeans.

HE RETURNED home and went up to the bedroom, where he put ten thousand dollars in an envelope he labeled *Thaddeus* and another ten in a separate envelope that he left unmarked. Then he took the remaining five thousand, put it in a third envelope, and went downstairs. There he found Sydney, kissed her, and told her he'd be back to take the family out to dinner. The boys had not yet come home.

Out on the street, he ignitioned his Edge.

ORNAZIAN DROVE to the District Line on Eleventh Street and parked his car. Michael was out on the side patio, splitting wood with a maul. A short man came out of a side door and said something to make Michael smile. Michael raised his arms and let the short man combinate a soft left and a right to his solar plexus. Michael took the punches and barely flinched. The two of them laughed and then the man began to gather the wood that Michael had split. Loaded with the fuel for the oven, the short man returned to the kitchen.

Watching Michael in his element, working and happy, Ornazian felt a flush of shame.

He found the envelope in his daypack, got out of his car, and walked toward the patio. Michael frowned as he approached.

"Hey," said Ornazian. "This is for you."

He handed Michael the envelope. Without looking at its contents, Michael slipped it under his shirt and apron.

"I guess that's it, then," said Michael. He placed the maul in a cage full of unsplit logs and fixed a padlock on its gate. He started to walk away.

"Hold on a second," said Ornazian.

"What?"

"Look…I never should have gotten you involved in this."

"You're comin to it a little late."

"I know. I was wrong. Accept my apology. Please."

Ornazian, blown and distraught, held out his hand. Michael hesitated. He was bitter, but it wouldn't cost him anything to give this man the small kindness he needed now.

Michael shook his hand.

"Thank you," said Ornazian.

Michael nodded, turned, and went through the side door that led to the kitchen. Ornazian stood there for a moment, then returned to his car.

HE LOWERED his window, rolled back the sunroof, and drove south on Eleventh to Lamont, then he hung a right, took a left on Sherman Avenue, and headed north.

I was wrong.

How had this happened?

It hadn't been his plan. No kid dreams of becoming corrupt. Ornazian tried to remember what had turned him, and he couldn't think of one event. A cop once told him that there were grass-eaters and meat-eaters on the force. A grass-eater accepts a free cup of coffee from a diner owner. A meat-eater takes the cup of coffee one day and demands protection money the next. With Ornazian, it was witness tampering. Then rip-and-runs. Home invasions. He'd told himself that he only took off bad people. He'd told himself the money was for his kids. For Sydney. For their future.

Well, he was done. He'd taken that ride and it was over. He didn't want his sons to know what their father was, and now they wouldn't know. If he and Sydney had to struggle financially, they'd struggle, but the boys would grow up with everything they needed: food, shelter, love, and, most important, two parents who set an example of how to live one's life.

He was headed home now. He'd kiss Gregg and Vic and hold them close as soon as he entered the house.

Up the road, a blue Mustang pulled off the curb and cut out in front of Ornazian. At Park Road and Sherman, Ornazian stopped at a red light behind the Mustang. Something about the car was familiar.

Ornazian glanced in his rearview mirror. A black Range Rover was accelerating toward him at high speed. It swerved around his Edge and came to an abrupt stop beside him.

He looked to his left, his heart beating rubbery in his chest. Cesar, Gustav's second, was in the passenger bucket of the Rover. A cut-down shotgun swung up in his hands.

Ornazian said, "Syd."

PART III

TWENTY-SIX

TEN MEN in orange jumpsuits sat in a circle in the chapel of the D.C. Jail. Anna, the jailhouse librarian, was among them. Two armed guards stood by, watching the proceedings but unconcerned, as there was rarely any trouble during the book club. In addition, the men in today's session were from the Fifty and Older unit, and were relatively docile. They were here because they wanted to be.

Anna had selected John D. MacDonald's *The Deep Blue Good-By*, the first novel in the Travis McGee series, originally published in 1964. Though it was at times a violent and erotic book, the sexual content was not graphic, and she had managed to get it in through the DCPL filter. Anna had argued that *The Deep Blue Good-By* was an important novel about the complex nature of masculinity and the cost of retribution. It was also a damned good read.

Most of the men had put the reading guide she had prepared under their chairs. Each man held a copy of the book, the twenty-third printing of a Fawcett Gold Medal paperback, in his hands. She had found copies in passable condition on the internet for next to nothing, all with the classic Ron Lesser cover art showing a woman with big hair wearing leopard-skin capri pants and high heels, her bare back exposed. Anna's father, recently diagnosed with colon cancer, had collected the McGee paperbacks. There always seemed to be one on his nightstand when she was growing up. So picking this book for the club had been an emotional choice as well as a literary one.

After a prayer, led by one of the more religious members of the group, the discussion commenced.

"What did you all think of the lead character, Travis McGee?" said Anna.

"That's a bad white boy right there," said a man named Sam, a serial parole violator with two clown patches of gray hair flanking a bald head. Anna never knew what Sam did to keep getting locked up, but it couldn't have been too egregious. He had a gentle manner.

"He's got no nine-to-five job," said Russell, an intelligent longtime heroin addict who dealt small quantities to pay for his habit. "He only works when he runs out of money. He's tall, strong, and good-looking. He can go with his hands. He drinks but he's not a drunk. He scores with all kinds of women. Got no commitments. No mortgage, no family. Shoot, the man lives on a houseboat. You don't get no freer than that."

"McGee is the man that many men would like to be," said Anna. "He's wish fulfillment in the flesh. That's one of the reasons the series was so popular."

"This reminded me of a Western movie," said a repeat offender named Randolph, a film freak who often spoke nostalgically about life in the 1970s, the decade, apparently, when he'd had the most fun. He was sixty years old, very tall, light-skinned with freckles, still wore his hair in a blowout, and had a comically long nose. Some of the men called him Big Bird.

"How so, Randolph?" said Anna.

"McGee is like John Wayne or some shit. You know that movie *The Searchers*? Ethan Edwards. That's McGee right there. He's a protector, but he don't fit into society nohow."

"He's more like a knight," said Russell, putting on his reading glasses and opening his book. "Look here, I marked it. Page twenty-nine. McGee talks about himself getting on his white steed, knocking the rust off his armor, and tilting a crooked old lance."

"There you go," said Sam. "The lance is crooked. That means Travis *knows* he's not straight."

"You could say he's a tarnished angel," said Anna. "What about the villain in the book, Junior Allen?"

The mention of Allen, the sociopathic predator of the novel, caused the group to stir.

"That's a wrong motherfucker right there," said a man. "Excuse me, Anna."

"McGee calls Junior a goat-god," said Russell. "A satyr."

"But isn't Junior similar, in a way, to McGee?" said Anna. "I'm talking about in their relations with women. Sure, Junior uses women for sport, but McGee also sleeps with many women he doesn't love."

"Ain't nothing wrong with that. A man got needs."

"Junior is like McGee if McGee was a bad person for real," said Russell.

"Junior is McGee's id," said Anna. "His dark side."

"That's why McGee got to kill him," said Russell, taking off his glasses and folding his hands in his lap.

"*Why* does he have to?" said Anna.

"So he can destroy that dark side of his self."

The men quietly considered that. Some of them nodded their heads.

"Someone should make a movie of this book," said a man.

"There was two Travis McGee movies," said Randolph.

"Now Randolph gonna school us about *cinema*," said Russell.

"One of 'em was a TV movie with a cowboy actor," said Randolph. "That don't even count. But there was one called *Darker than Amber*, with Rod Taylor as McGee? Taylor was macho, boy, he played the *shit* out of that role. There was like a ten-minute hand-to-hand fight in the end between him and William Smith, big muscle-bound cat who usually played bikers. It looked like the two of them were really going at it. The director was the same guy who did *Enter the Dragon*."

"Man, nobody ask you to talk about Bruce Lee. This is a book club, not a movie club."

"Just sayin," said Randolph. "*Darker than Amber* was tight. I saw it at the Booker T. back in the day."

"We ain't back in the motherfuckin day, Big Bird. So you can just step out of your time machine."

Laughter rippled through the group. Some of the men touched fists.

"Did John MacDonald make much money?" said a man.

The conversation and debate grew heated and lively. When it was time to end the session, many of the men wanted to stay.

"That was a good book," said Sam.

"Thank you, Miss Anna," said Russell.

"It was my pleasure," she said.

* * *

IN THE weeks that followed the murder of Phil Ornazian, Thaddeus Ward kept a low profile. He attended the funeral but did not speak to Ornazian's widow, Sydney, who never once looked his way. Ornazian's sons were not there. His wife, apparently, had spared them the sight of their father's casket being lowered into the ground.

Ward checked into his business, Ward Bonds, infrequently. In his absence, he had put Genesis, the smart ex–National Guardswoman, in charge. She was a natural manager and was good with the clientele.

At home, he drew the curtains, placed loaded guns in various rooms, and kept his shotgun by his bed. He told his daughter not to visit, that he would come see her and his grandchildren when the opportunity arose. If the killers were going to come for him, he would be ready, but he would be ready alone.

They didn't come.

Restless, he drove into Northwest one day and found the garage in the alley near Kansas Avenue where Ornazian had gotten his hacks. There he met Berhanu, an Ethiopian with curly black hair, in one of the bays. It had come to Ward that the cameras on the brothel's street had recorded the Impala SS they had used in the robbery.

The Impala was not here, but there were three high-horse imports in the garage. After introducing himself, Ward asked Berhanu, known by many in this part of the city as an off-the-books renter of cars, if anyone had come to him asking about the renter of the SS. Berhanu told him that a Spanish man with

251

a clean-shaven face had done just that, but he added that he had not given the man any information. Ward believed him.

"Anybody work here with you?" said Ward.

"I had a man," said Berhanu. "A mechanic named Donnie. But he's gone."

"What do you mean, gone?"

"He didn't show up for work one day and never returned. I left messages, but…" Berhanu shrugged. "Donnie was a drunk. Good with tools, but unreliable."

Ward considered this. In his heart he knew that it was Gustav who had ordered the hit on Ornazian. It fit that the mechanic had given up the plate numbers on Ornazian's Ford in exchange for a payoff. It would be simple to locate the Ornazian residence and follow Phil from there. They'd executed the classic trap at the intersection of Park and Sherman. Cesar, most likely, had wielded the shotgun that ended Phil's life.

Nos encontraremos otra vez.

We will meet another time.

It was the last thing Cesar had said to them the night they'd bound him to a chair. He'd made good on his promise.

"I'm sorry about Phil," said Berhanu. "I liked him."

"So did I," said Ward.

The question for Ward was, what would he do now? Homicide detectives had already shown up at his house and spoken to him. He imagined that Sydney had given him up as a business associate. Ward, despite his past as a D.C. cop, had told them he had no knowledge of the event. His involvement in the home invasion would have incriminated him, of course, but there was something else. In the image he had of himself, he saw retaliation, some payback for the murder of his friend.

Soon after his meeting with Berhanu, Sydney called Ward on his cell and asked if he could meet her at a spot in her neighborhood.

They sat at a booth at Slim's, a diner on Georgia and Upshur. Both of them were drinking coffee. Sydney's cheeks were drawn. She appeared to have lost weight. Her body odor was strong. He wondered when she had showered last.

"I have something for you," she said, and she reached into her bag. She found an envelope and dropped it on the table between them. *Thaddeus* was written across the face of the envelope in Phil Ornazian's scrawl. Ward took it and slipped it into the inside pocket of his jacket.

"Aren't you going to count it?" said Sydney. "There's ten thousand dollars in there."

"I don't need to count it."

"Was it worth it?"

"Of course not," he said. "Look, I'm sorry."

"I don't want your apology. I only came here to give you your money. Do you know why? Because Phil would have wanted me to. In his own way, he was an honorable man."

"I'll gladly give you this money back. It's the least I can do."

"No need. Phil took care of everything. He had a half-million-dollar life insurance policy. On top of that, unbeknownst to me, he had taken out mortgage insurance so that in the event of his death, our house would be paid for. If you don't account for the fact that I no longer have a husband and my sons will grow up without a father, everything's just fine."

"I'm sorry," said Ward, again, because he could think of nothing else to say.

"I blame myself, not you. I knew that the two of you were into something wrong. I told Phil that I didn't like it. That I was afraid for him. I told him gently. But I should have threatened to leave him if he continued on with whatever he was doing. I should have screamed it into his face."

"I'm going to find the ones—"

"No!" she said, loud enough to turn heads in the diner. "*No.* Just stop it, Thaddeus. This has to stop." She gathered herself. "Answer me one question: Are my children safe? Are the people who did this going to do violence to me and my family?"

"This wasn't about retrieving what we took from them. It was about revenge. I've thought hard about this. They're not going to do anything to an innocent woman and her children. It's too high-profile. It will bring all kinds of heat down on them." He held her gaze while she stared back at him, quiet anger radiating off her. "The answer is, you and the kids are safe."

She stood up abruptly and left him there. He watched her through the window as she walked east on Upshur. Their waitress came and asked him if everything was all right. He told her he was fine.

Stop.

Sydney was right. They had played a bold game and paid a price. The only thing left was more bloodshed. More loss. And anyway, he was damn near seventy years old. It was time to get off the stage.

Ward was done.

TWENTY-SEVEN

LATE IN the spring, Michael Hudson convinced his mother that their dog Brandy's time had come. Brandy had long been unable to climb stairs, and now she dragged her rear feet when she went to the front door to bark at the mailman, Gerard, or when she tried to walk to her dish come feeding time. Michael sat his mother down and gently explained to her that it was selfish and cruel to prolong the life of an animal that was suffering. She agreed to have Brandy euthanized.

Brandy was on her bed by the couch with her favorite ball and rubber bone next to her as their vet injected a solution into her paw. Doretha Hudson talked to her and rubbed behind her ear in that spot that made her sigh as the pentobarbital took effect, rendering her unconscious and shutting down her heart and brain. She was looking up at Michael, seated beside her on the floor, as the light left her eyes.

The very next day Michael and his mother went to the shelter on Blair Road and Oglethorpe Street, as they had done when he was in high school, and found a dog. It was not a puppy but an adult terrier mix. Not big or strong, and not all that attractive, but with lively eyes. As they approached him, he came up off his bed, put his feet up on the door of his space, and licked Doretha's outstretched hand. His tail wagged furiously.

"That's the one," said Doretha.

"Kinda funny lookin," said Michael. "There's plenty of cute puppies here we could get."

"Everybody wants a puppy. This dog here won't get adopted unless we take him home. I like him."

"What about that name?" said Michael. The card on the door said the dog's name was Honeyboy.

"I'm going to call him O'Jay."

"You gonna name him after a murderer? For real?"

"Not for O. J. Simpson, silly. Brandy was named for that beautiful O'Jays song about a man who's missing his dog. So I'm just making a connection." Doretha smiled. "Let's go talk to that nice Spanish girl and do the paperwork."

There was a dark-haired young lady named Rosa who worked at the shelter and who had been very helpful when they arrived.

"She's Guatemalan," said Michael.

"So? The point is, Michael, let's take O'Jay home."

"Whatever you want, Mama." He meant it too.

MICHAEL HAD begun to spend the money a little at a time. He used it to get a new pair of Timbs, and a Helly Hansen jacket from a shop at Gallery Place, but he was not much of a clotheshorse, and he needed little for himself. He found a bookcase with glass doors at an antique spot on North Capitol Street, splurged on that and a cab ride home, and put it up in his room. He bought more books.

Mostly, he used the money on others. He bought one of those comfortable outdoor chairs, the weather-resistant kind people put on decks, for Woods, the veteran amputee who was usually out back in the alley. He didn't like seeing Woods sitting on an overturned crate. And he bought Alisha, Carla Thomas's daughter, a set of children's books recommended by the lady at the store on Upshur Street. It wasn't going anywhere with Carla, but they were friends, and he liked her little girl.

One night he took his mother out to dinner at the Prime Rib on K Street because she had always wanted to go. He asked for a table near the piano where they could hear the man in his tuxedo play and sing standards and watch the bar, where nice-looking people drank and socialized. His mother had the signature dish that gave the establishment its name, and he had a New York strip, medium rare. The atmosphere and service were impeccable, which Michael, now in the restaurant business, could appreciate. His mother was in her glory.

The money would soon be gone. It wasn't much to begin with, not by modern standards. Not enough to have risked death, of that he was certain. Michael thought of this every time he walked to work and passed the intersection of Park and Sherman, where Phil Ornazian had been murdered in his car.

With everything that had happened, there was a lesson to be learned, and Michael had taken it to heart. He was alive, and he was straight.

* * *

HIS JOB at the District Line was secure. It was not a challenging position, but it was work, and he was accepted and had found a second family there. Despite Angelos Valis's frequent reminders that Michael would receive a raise only when the minimum wage went up, he was in fact given a raise, unceremoniously. The increase simply showed up one Friday in his paycheck. Also, he had health insurance. It looked like he had a home here for as long as he wanted it. All was fine, for now.

But he was looking ahead. He had spoken to Gerard again about a U.S. Postal Service job, and he had downloaded a sample of the 473E, the entrance exam. It was mostly memory questions, numbers, codes, addresses, routes, stuff like that. He was confident that he could score high. The criminal background check could present a problem, but he planned to visit his lawyer, Mr. Mirapaul, to see about the juvenile priors and the adult charges that were still on his record. Maybe Mr. Mirapaul could help him get those things expunged. It would take time. But that was all right.

It wasn't just the U.S. Postal Service job that made him want to clear his record. He wanted to do volunteer stuff, too, and that would involve working with kids. He had other ideas as well. If he enrolled and took some college classes, maybe starting at UDC or Montgomery College, over the Maryland line, he might get the ambition to keep going with it and earn his degree. Maybe teach, eventually. Teach about books.

It was possible. It *was*.

* * *

ONE EVENING, coming out of Wall of Books on Georgia Avenue, Michael saw Anna and her husband seated at one of the outdoor picnic tables at the Midlands, having a talk. They looked serious. Her husband, Rick was his name, was wearing a hat that said TITLEIST across the front. He was drinking a beer. Anna was drinking water.

Michael didn't walk over to the patio to say hello. It looked like they were discussing something important, and he didn't want to bother them. Though he thought of her often, he hadn't seen Anna or talked to her for quite a while. He had walked up to her neighborhood a couple of times in the past month, watched the soccer games at the rec center there, in the hopes that she'd come past on her bike. But she hadn't, and it was better that way. He didn't know what he wanted, but he knew that trying to take things further with her was wrong.

He had no desire to upend her life. But he missed her.

THE NEXT time he ran into Anna was during the dinner rush at the restaurant. She was picking up a pizza to take out, and he was delivering glassware to the bar. She was by the cash register, and she saw him and smiled. He walked along the bar until he came to where she stood.

"Anna."

"Michael. How's it going?"

"A little warm down there in the kitchen. But I'm fine. About to be the best dishwasher in the city, if I keep this up."

"Is it a contest?"

"In a way. How have you been?"

"I'm still at the jail. We have an actual library there now, where the inmates can browse for books. Everything's good."

For a moment, neither of them spoke. He looked into her eyes.

"Seriously," she said. "Are you doing all right?"

"I am. I'm thinking of enrolling in a couple of college courses. Like English. But it's a blessing to have this job right here too." His expression grew serious. "I don't know. Maybe I'll buy a farm out in the country, something like that. 'An' live off the fatta the lan'.'"

Anna laughed. "You remembered."

"How could I forget?" he said. "You've still got my number, right?"

"Yes. And you have mine."

"You ever need anything, Anna, all you got to do is hit me up. You got a friend in this city, hear? For life."

"As do you," she said.

"Be easy, Anna."

Michael turned and headed for the spiral stairs.

ANNA WALKED home slowly, because she needed the time alone.

She was pregnant.

The next time Michael would see her, she'd be showing, or maybe she'd be out on the patio of the District Line with her husband and their baby. A stroller by their table, like so many others. Like all the young couples who had taken that next step.

Rick, once a die-hard stay-in-the-city enthusiast, had already begun to talk about putting their house on the market and buying something bigger, with "more yard" and space "for the kid to play," in Maryland or Northern Virginia. Someplace near a golf course, no doubt. She'd end up compromising. It was a partnership. It wasn't all about only what she wanted or liked.

She wasn't unhappy. She knew she'd love her child and she wanted to be a good parent, as her own parents had been. And yet these things that were being put in motion couldn't be reversed. She could see her trajectory.

Her mood lightened as she thought of tomorrow. Not the long tomorrow, but the immediate days that were to come. She was preparing for the next book club and had staged the cart for the Gen Pop unit the following day. There was a young man named Terrell in Gen Pop who had shown a growing interest in reading. She had chosen something especially for him, a positive memoir about growing up on the once-notorious block of Hanover Place, a book called *Slugg*, by Tony Lewis Jr. She felt certain that Terrell would like it.

Not everything was perfect, or would be. Anna was married to a good man she loved, and together they would make a family. She had her work. And a friend in the city, for life.

IN HIS spare time, Michael Hudson had begun to venture out of his neighborhood and his quadrant to explore the wider city around him. He visited the renovated Mount Pleasant library, which held fifty thousand books, and the beautiful Francis Gregory Library, in Ward 7, designed by David Adjaye. At various libraries, Michael signed up for discussion groups and attended movie nights. And, for the first time in his life, he took advantage of the numerous world-class art galleries and museums in D.C. to which entry was free. He was growing.

On a day in early summer, as dark afternoon clouds began to gather, he walked to Petworth to pick up a novel he had ordered from the store on Upshur Street. The book was *True Grit.* Anna had recommended it to him when he was incarcerated. She knew he liked Westerns, and this one, she'd said, was a classic.

He paid for the book, an Overland Press trade edition, and found a seat on a bench. He opened the novel and read the first paragraph.

People do not give it credence that a fourteen-year-old girl could leave home and go off in the wintertime to avenge her father's blood but it did not seem so strange then, although I will say it did not happen every day. I was just fourteen years of age when a coward going by the name of Tom Chaney shot my father down in Fort Smith, Arkansas, and robbed him of his life and his horse and $150 in cash money plus two California gold pieces that he carried in his trouser band.

Michael closed the book and rubbed his thumb across its cover.

The clouds broke and drops began to fall. He was not near shelter, so he decided it was best to head home. Michael slid the book into his shirt, adjusted the watch cap that was on his head, and went south on foot. He was already thinking about the book, its marriage of story and voice. It had captured him immediately. It had taken him somewhere else.

To anyone watching, he was one of many out on the street, going along, stepping quick against the weather. They couldn't know his inner life, or his history, or that he was a Washingtonian, born and bred, with a steady job, family and friends. A lover of books. A man who knew who he was and who he hoped to be.

Just another man who came uptown.

Walking in the rain.

ACKNOWLEDGMENTS

Thanks to Danielle Zoller, Dave Constantine, Linnea Hegarty, Margaret Goodbody, Frazier O'Leary, Joe Aronstamn, Jon Norris, Betsy Willeford, Gerard Young, Paul Ruppert, Rick Kain, Mark Billingham, and the many inmates of the D.C. Jail who have let me into their world over the years. I would also like to thank Reagan Arthur, Katharine Myers, Betsy Uhrig, and Sabrina Callahan of Little, Brown; Josh Kendall of Mulholland Books; Emad Akhtar of Orion in the UK; Robert Pépin of Calmann-Lévy in France; and Sloan Harris.

The following organizations do good work and often change lives: the Free Minds Book Club, the PEN/Faulkner Foundation Writers in Schools program, the D.C. Public Library Foundation, the Innocence Project, and Open City Advocates. Check them out online if you'd like to get involved.

As always, a shout-out to the readers. I appreciate you.